NICHOLAS COFFIN: THE ALCHEMIST

Borgia spun on his heel and stalked away from the fireplace, then back. His head was held low as he walked and his eyes burned golden from under his brows. His voice tight, he regarded Coffin level- ly. "You say it was poison. I have the resources to make you tell me all the rest you know."

"I know."

"You don't seem to realize it," Borgia said, "but I am the most dangerous man in Rome."

"I know."

"Then what makes you stand there facing me? I could have you untied sinew by sinew. What do you have for a defense against me?"

"Knowledge," Coffin answered quietly.

THE Alchemist:
DEATH OF A BORGIA

C. J. STEVERMER

CHARTER
NEW YORK

A DIVISION OF CHARTER COMMUNICATIONS INC.
A GROSSET & DUNLAP COMPANY

THE ALCHEMIST: DEATH OF A BORGIA
Copyright © 1980 by C. J. Stevermer

A Charter Original.

First Charter Printing January 1981
Published simultaneously in Canada
Manufactured in the United States of America

2 4 6 8 0 9 7 5 3 1

One for the money.
And for John, Carol,
Ellen and Robert.

THE Alchemist:
DEATH OF A BORGIA

CHAPTER ONE

"How rude of me," the young man remarked, closing the door behind him, "to be late for dinner, when I am your only guest."

His hostess eyed him calmly from the window seat across the dining room. Behind her, the chill of the Roman night was kept out by brocade curtains, elaborately figured, but her own figure was elaborate enough to more than hold his gaze.

"Disgraceful behavior," she said, and set aside the lute she had been toying with. "As disgraceful as my own. I pray you will forgive me, my dear, but I have planned only a very simple meal for us this evening. No musicians, no entertainment, only a few dishes. I hoped to entertain you with simplicity."

"How novel." The young man, severely clad in black velvet, crossed the room to take her hand in his. Despite the chill, she wore her gold brocade gown over a chemise of sheerest white gossamer silk, cut to accent the swan's curve of her throat and nearly bare her shoulders. He surveyed the result with satisfaction. "No pretty youths sawing on their viols? No plump little dancers strutting between courses? No mechanical owls?"

"None."

"How refreshing," he said, as he led her to her place at the head of the table.

"I thought you might enjoy a change," she answered. "Observe how I create the effect of rusticity: not silver goblets, but Venetian glass, not chased silver plates, but glazed earthenware cleverly designed, and not an enameled salt cellar, but simply a polished seashell."

The fair-haired youth took his seat opposite her. "It might have been made for me alone."

"Precisely the effect I'd hoped to achieve," she replied. With a sharp clap of her slender hands, she summoned the serving man.

"So," her guest said, as the plump servant appeared at his mistress' side with a silver tray, "we shall be as simple as peasants this evening."

"Not quite that simple, I trust. Duccio, sip the wine before you taste the first course, so that my lord may have a glass while we wait for your decision on the seafood," the dark-haired woman requested. Her servant nodded and poured out a glass of wine to sip while she took a small silver porringer from the tray and filled it with a portion of the dish he had brought in, mussels in a savory wine sauce. When the wine was half gone, he smiled his approval, then turned his attention to the seafood. He chewed and swallowed with great concentration for several moments, then ran his forefinger across the bottom of the dish and licked the tip thoughtfully.

"It tastes fine to me, madonna, but perhaps you would like me to taste some more to be perfectly certain?" he asked, his voice filled with anticipation.

"Thank you, Duccio," she responded, pouring out her guest's wine herself. "I think that will be unnecessary. You may serve us."

Deftly, the servant poured forth her wine and spooned out seafood onto their painted plates, then bowed and retreated, taking his tray with him.

The blond youth lifted his wineglass in a salute to his hostess, took a sip, and said, "Tell me, how does he know if he's been poisoned? As many times as I have dined here, I've never been able to catch him doing more than stare at the ceiling. After a few minutes, he tells you the food is fine and hints for more, and then he goes on serving. If he were poisoned, he'd have no idea whether it was in the wine or the food."

"It makes no matter to me how he identifies the poison so long as he finds it," she answered. "Our inefficient attitude must annoy you, I feel certain, but not everyone shares your family's enthusiasm for these matters."

"May I, for one evening," he asked crisply, "be allowed to forget my family?"

She paled and looked down at her plate in silence for a moment, then said huskily, "I have displeased you."

He watched her pleat the table damask with little

abrupt pinches of her thumb and forefinger. After another sip of the pale wine, he spoke.

"In my turn, I have displeased you. Let us forget the matter. I have been hard-pressed of late, but you have done nothing but study how to please me. Forgive me, and I forgive you."

"Done," she answered.

"Only one thing," he added plaintively. "Do not ask me to go through my speech. I've been through it twice today. Once more and I will lose all my appetite."

"If you insist," she agreed, with a tilt of her head. "But what if you have not practiced it enough?"

"Then I will stumble through it and rely on the menu to distract my audience from my mistakes."

"Good strategy." She clapped her hands again and Duccio appeared, bearing the second course. With dispatch, the sampling took place and the wine was replenished; then partridge in a sweet sauce was set before them, and the plump servant retired. Before they could continue, however, the youth drew a black silk packet from the breast of his doublet.

"While you use this to distract me," he said, unfolding the black silk, "allow me to distract you."

Nestled in the silk was a brooch centered with a square-cut ruby the size of a man's thumbnail. The stone flashed scarlet as it was passed across the table and pressed into her hands. She made a silent "oh" with her carefully carmined lips as she lifted the jewel and let it glitter in the candlelight. With one long fingernail she tapped the baroque pearl dangling beneath the ruby, then ran a fingertip along the goldwork of the setting.

"My friend," she said huskily, "you are indeed generous. And this strategy is most effective as a distraction. But if you follow it among all the guests at your banquet tomorrow, I fear it will pauper you."

"I have no intention of being such a spendthrift, though perhaps the cost would be small compared to the labor of learning a Latin oration. No, this trifle is just for you. I think I know you well enough to guess what will please you."

"Oh, yes," she sighed. "It is perfection. Yet I cannot think of any occasion to warrant such a gift."

"No occasion. I wanted to see you smile," he replied.

She did so, brilliantly; then with a practiced motion she centered the brooch at her neckline and pinned it carefully in place. It pulsed gently there with the steady rise and fall of her breasts and her guest observed it appreciatively.

"Rubies suit you," he decided. "I must give you more of them."

"And get more smiles in return?" she asked. "The market will decline, will it not, for where there are so many smiles, the price must decrease."

"What, am I a merchant?" he chided her, adroitly boning his partridge. "Shall I hedge the market, and go from rubies to carnelians and then to garnets?"

"Why stop there? You still have red paste gems and window glass to choose from, and one day you may be so weary of my smile you'll give me bricks," she retorted.

"I may, but I know you well enough to expect to get them back again with gusto, and I have no desire to let my mistress hurl bricks at my head," he replied.

"Oh, but you're safe from that. It's rude to return a gift," she pointed out, and refilled his wine glass.

When the partridge was eaten and the third course summoned, Duccio rejoined them. The wine and entree, this time roast mutton, were sampled and pronounced palatable. Then the plump servant circled the table, clearing up crumbs and unwanted serving pieces. After hovering for several moments, he succeeded in capturing his employer's attention.

"Yes, Duccio? Is something troubling you?"

"No, madonna, not me. Only I feel I have to warn you that the cook let the oven get a bit hot, and the little almond cakes you planned are quite burnt."

"How tiresome," she said. "Very well, then. This will be our last course, Duccio. There will be no need to return until my lord and I have finished. Clear up after we leave the table."

"Very well, madonna," Duccio replied, then bowed himself and his tray out of the room.

"My apologies, my dear. I will have an ice to make up for it next time we dine together," she promised, then looked more closely at her companion. "My dear," she said sharply, "you are quite pale. Is something wrong?"

"No, not in the least." The young man had gone very white and was breathing quickly and shallowly.

"Nonsense. You are eyeing that mutton as though it were a snake. It will be taken away at once."

"No, please. It's not the mutton—" he broke off and rubbed his forehead, then blinked. "I like mutton. It's just that I feel a bit strange. Only a headache, I suppose. Please don't trouble yourself."

"But I know a certain cure for the headache," she answered, pushing her plate away. "I'll order my maid to warm the sheets."

Despite his protests, she left him briefly to find the maid and issue orders. When she returned he had drained his wineglass and gotten some of his color back. He rose as she entered and held out a hand.

"That's better," she said approvingly, taking the hand he offered. They stood close for a moment. "The air is stale here, perhaps. We will do very well in another room."

"An excellent notion," he said, as he reached to touch the brooch at her décolletage. "What chamber shall we choose?"

"My maid is only warming one pair of sheets."

"Lead me to them, then," he requested.

But their progress up the stair robbed him of the color he had regained and left him paler than before and breathing raggedly. Perfectly composed, his mistress called for a basin and helped him to the bed. The basin arrived as she lifted his booted legs on the bed so he could recline.

"Take that thing away," he began weakly.

"Leave it," she told her maid, her voice crisp and calm. "Now then—"

The maid closed the door behind her and the two were left alone. Working quickly, she loosened his doublet and shirt at the throat and sponged his forehead with cool water, although her fingers told her he was chilled.

"No need to fuss," he protested. "I drank a lot of wine, that's all." A wave of nausea caught him before he could go on.

She held his head as he used the basin, then helped him wipe his mouth and settle back on the pillows.

"That's better," he said. "I'm terribly sorry. I just overindulged and now you have to pay the price. Too much wine, too much good food—I do apologize, my dear."

"How do you feel now?" she asked, waving aside his protests and acknowledging his apologies with a nod. She touched his forehead anxiously. "You're still so pale."

"I'll be better soon," he assured her. "Call someone to take that basin away and help me with my boots and I'll show you how much better."

At her call, the maid returned to whisk the basin out of the bedchamber. When she was gone, the worried woman turned back to her lover, ready to take off his boots herself. To her alarm, his eyes were closed and he lay limp and bloodless. She moved to kneel beside him with an involuntary cry, groping under his doublet for a heartbeat. Just as her slender hand touched the clammy skin beneath his linen shirt, he opened his eyes and folded his arms around her to hold her close.

"Fooled you," he said, drawing her head down to his shoulder.

Hearing the light, swift heartbeat as she leaned on his shoulder, and feeling his chill skin under her fingertips, she did not speak, but a vertical line appeared between her perfectly plucked dark eyebrows.

For a few minutes they were still, she kneeling beside the bed encircled by his arms, he stretched full length on the thick feather bed. Then, with small gentle strokes, he began to smooth her hair, pausing now and then to take out one of her golden hairpins. She lay still and let him take down the dark coils of her hair, strewing the pins across the counterpane and pillows. To her, it seemed incredible that his arms could have lost so much strength, for when he had put them around her, she had felt how they trembled. Now he seemed to have recovered somewhat, but she still pressed her ear against his shoulder and her hand against his chest. His heartbeat still raced and his breathing, was, if anything, shallower than before. His pallor had taken on a tinge of blue. Cold against her cheek, his fingers began to tremble as he stroked her silken hair. She took his hand in her warm one and moved it to her lips.

Without warning his hand clenched into a fist and he rolled away from her onto his side, half convulsed with cramps. His strangled moan brought her to her feet in a single fluid motion and sent her halfway across the room, calling for her maid. His second groan stopped her and brought her back to his side, and the third was little more than a tearing, bubbling gasp. She drew him into her arms and pressed her mouth against his, attempting to share her breath with him. Muscle spasms racked his frame, while his frightened, lucid eyes were locked with hers. She moved her head to allow him to exhale, but his breath rattled out with an unnatural sound like a sheet ripping. Doggedly, she forced another breath from her lungs into his, and tightened her arms around his chest to help him exhale it, dreading the tearing sound of his breathing. The rattle came again, longer this time, and she forced herself to face him again, preparing another stolen breath. Before she could part her lips, she realized his open eyes could not see her any longer, and that the fluttering heartbeat under her hands had stopped.

At last a timid knock came at the door.

"Madonna?" her maid called. "Did you wish for me, madonna?"

She rose stiffly to her feet and took a last look at what had lain heavily in her arms, then drew the brocade curtains closed around the bed. With a slow tread, she walked to the door and opened it.

"I called," she said to the maid, "but I do not need you now. Go to bed. I will have you attend me in the morning."

"Very well, madonna." The maid curtsied and turned to go.

The mistress closed the door and went back to the bed, parted the curtains and gazed in steadily. Again, the vertical line appeared between her brows, marring the perfection of her face. Lost in thought, she went on gazing. There was much to be planned before morning.

CHAPTER TWO

From his window, Nicholas Coffin could see just enough of the garden to wonder why he had ever come to Rome. The green-black cypress never changed a whit, not even in January's chill. The stiff and fragmented statues gleamed white in the moonlight. Coffin looked down into the darkness, where a single marble arm rose up out of shadow, brandishing a bunch of marble grapes. He shook his head. Not a tree limb, not a blade of grass, had changed since his arrival in Rome the year before. Back home, the year had swung full circle: snow to rain, rain to mist, mist to the full glory of English summer, summer to crisp autumn, and autumn rain back to snow at the year's end. Morton Hempstead would look tonight much as he remembered leaving it the year before, and soon, the season would turn again; the frost in the earth would give way to spring. In Rome, the change would only be in greater danger from the plague-ridden

Pontine marshes. The days would be mild, then warm, then hot, then damned unhealthy—and all the while that idiotic statue would hold high that bunch of grapes. Coffin shook his head again, despairingly.

The wind shifted, and brought with it enough chill to make him draw on his jerkin and lace it. Coffin swung the shutters closed and turned back to his books. Best to finish while he could work undistracted, he told himself. Then, when she arrived, he could devote his entire attention to her.

Before he had opened a book, he heard the pounding at the door.

Coffin opened the door, looked out and then down into a grimy face.

"Oh, Angelo—" his voice betrayed his disappointment. "I wasn't expecting you. Er, good evening."

As Angelo stepped across the threshold into the lamplight, Coffin added in mild surprise, "You're wet, Angelo."

"I know," Angelo responded. "Think nothing of it. Please come with me, Maestro. I've found something for you."

"In whose pocket?" Coffin asked, without reflection.

"No, no. You misunderstand. I've found something you *need*."

The little man bounced slightly to convey his urgency.

"No one needs anything badly enough to go out at this hour. It's midnight, Angelo. I couldn't leave even if I wanted to. I'm expecting my—a friend."

"Oh, a woman." Comprehension brightened Angelo's dirty face. "I understand. Women are very important, I agree. But this has to do with your work, signore."

Coffin ran his fingers through his hair, leaving it like dark, ruffled plumage.

"Angelo, I doubt you are much involved with my concerns, or know anything of my work. I am a scholar."

"All Englishmen say that. They come to Rome to study in her great libraries. *Basta!* They spend more time studying wineshops and expensive women. No wonder they say an Englishman italianate is the devil incarnate. And you, Maestro Coffin, study alchemy, do you not? Casting spells, turning lead into gold—well, I have something you need."

"It had better be the philosopher's stone itself, Angelo, or I'm locking the door," warned Coffin.

"Enough of subtlety, then. You want a body, Maestro?" Angelo threw open his stubby hands. "I've got one for you. Don't look so startled. You're an alchemist, aren't you? Bat's tongues, virgin's hair. . . . Isn't that why you study those books all the time?"

"I am an alchemist," Coffin protested, "I am not a ghoul."

"I know, Maestro, you are a gentleman and you have your studies." Angelo said soothingly. "You cast spells, you need these things. Virgin's hair, dead men's eyes. . . . Not that I'm saying he's a virgin, mind, but he's certainly dead. Oh, he's a beau-

ty, signore, and fresh as a new-caught fish from the
river. I saw him float by, there in the moonlight,
and thought of you."

"Very kind, Angelo, but I do not cast spells on
people. I do not cut them up for spare parts. I
study the elements and seek to refine them into
their original components. Knowledge, that's what
I'm after, not a rotting corpse."

"Just wait until you see him. Rotting indeed.
Didn't I tell you he was fresh? Take one look, and
if you don't like, I'll throw him right back where I
found him, and a fine waste it will be, too."

"You're generous," Coffin said, drily. "But I really cannot go out tonight. If he's so valuable, why
in hell can't you bring him here?"

"He's on the landing, Maestro," said Angelo.
"It will only take a moment."

"God's bones, man! This isn't the dark ages! It's
1501! You can't go about carrying bodies through
the streets!"

"Nobody noticed me. And a moment ago you
would have sent me out after it yourself," the little
man protested.

"Well, as long as you've brought him as far as
the stairs, you'd better get him inside before anyone sees." Coffin's lean face was grim.

"Don't be angry, signore. I promise he wan't
bleeding. Anyway, how could I leave him in the
street, eh? Rome is full of thieves. No sooner would
I turn my back than someone would make off with
him. Such bodies as this one are not found every
night."

The little man bounced down the stairs, to reappear shortly, half-hidden by the dripping man slung round his shoulders. He and his burden trickled their way across to a narrow bed. A noise of irritation from Coffin stopped him halfway there.

"Not there, idiot. In the next room."

Knees prominently abuckle, Angelo trudged into the workroom and deposited the body on the large table. Coffin followed, candle in hand. Angelo stood back. The corpse lay supine, right arm pointing limply down to the clean-scrubbed tile floor.

Both men stared speechlessly at what the candlelight revealed. After a moment, Angelo broke the silence.

"Santa Maria! He's blue!"

Without thinking, Coffin lifted the dangling arm and folded it right hand over left on the dead man's chest. Both hands were mutilated, each missing the last two fingers, but little blood was in evidence. Hands, face, throat: all were tinged a pale, sickish shade of blue. The face was a darker shade than the hands, but both hands and face were aristocratically slender. The man's hair and beard were blond, still damp. His clothes were expensive but severely simple.

Coffin turned back to Angelo, eyes ablaze.

"Where did you get him?" he demanded.

"I found him, just as I said," Angelo answered plaintively. "In the river."

"Where were you?"

"On the bridge," the little man replied.

"And by the light of the moon you detected a corpse floating past? He must have been walking on the water for you to have seen him tonight," Coffin retorted.

"No, Maestro. It is as I said. I heard a sound and when I looked toward it, I saw the darkness of its shape in the water."

"A sound?" Coffin asked, his voice a purr.

"Yes, a splashing noise."

"Oh, and when you looked toward the noise, you saw something dark in the water."

"And knowing you would pay me well, Maestro, I went to get it."

"Pay you for what, Angelo?" asked Coffin.

"Why, for the body, sir."

"How astute of you to guess it was a body. You couldn't have seen much of it after it hit the water." Coffin's voice went from a purr to a rasp. "Tell me *all* you saw, Angelo."

Angelo blanched as he looked into the Englishman's eyes.

"Yes, Signore Coffin. As you say. I was on the bridge."

"Which bridge?" demanded Coffin.

"The one beneath the Palatino. Just upstream from here."

"Good. Go on." Coffin's voice was soft again.

"Yes, signore." Angelo winced. "Times haven't been so good lately. People don't go out late this time of year. Not rich ones, anyway. But I was waiting below the hill, to greet the bold of heart and heavy of purse. From the bridge, I could see a good way up the Tevere, up to an alley mouth on the Palatine side, down close to the water. There were two of them, with this one between them. I could just make them out in the moonlight. They had bright cloaks on, so they must not have been professionals. When they got this fellow down to the river, they dropped him in and ran. I stood there and watched it bob toward me."

"With a headful of fancy stories about alchemy, I expect." Coffin said dryly. Ignoring him, Angelo went on.

"When it came close enough, I fished it out."

"Which is how you got so wet," finished Coffin. "That's better, Angelo."

"It's what I said before."

"You left out the important part before. Someone wanted to dispose of that body quickly and they were in such a rush they simply dragged it to the river and dropped it in. I wonder why?"

"Because they killed him and didn't want to be caught," Angelo said, prosaically. "Or maybe because he was blue."

"I mean, why kill him? And how?" Coffin turned back to the body, eyes ablaze. "How?"

Grateful to have the alchemist's attention shift back to the body, Angelo heaved a sigh and looked about him for the first time. Shelves lined the walls, filled with glassware of arcane shape and unknown purpose, crocks sealed to hold God knew what, and a few books whose worn spines proclaimed them of little value to a man in Angelo's profession.

"So this is where you do it," he marveled. "Funny, it looks just like an apothecary's."

"It looks just like a charnel-house now, thanks to you."

Coffin turned to a shelf and reached for his scalpel in its leather case. Angelo stepped forward, hand outstretched. Coffin looked up from the body, surprised.

"It is as I said, is it not? He's fresh. If you like, I will leave him. Then it will be cash before you cut. If not, back to the river he goes."

"I should send him back with you," Coffin scowled. "What's your price?"

"To leave him here? Twenty crowns." Angelo smiled affably. "To take him back to the river? That will cost more."

Angelo's voice trailed off before Coffin's withering gaze.

"Since you've already had a slice at him to steal the rings he was wearing, you'll have to settle for less. Damaged merchandise, don't you know? For example, I'll never get a Hand of Glory out of a corpse lacking fingers. The value goes down right there. So I think you'll agree," Coffin's pleasant voice was belied by the hardness in his eyes, "that I'm the best judge of the going rate."

Coffin turned to a shelf behind him and lifted a small casket, locked and bound with iron. When he set it on the table, it produced a small, satisfying chink of coins sliding within. Coffin fumbled in his doublet for the key.

"Allow me, sir," Angelo stepped up to the table, withdrawing a long sliver of metal from his pouch.

"Just between friends, I don't mind letting you watch, Maestro Coffin, but I'd hate to let a rival see my technique."

He inserted the splinter of metal into the lock and twisted. The lock snapped open.

"Between friends, Angelo," Coffin commented acidly, "I don't mind watching your technique. In the future, however, be warned. I will find a better lock."

"Oh, you needn't fear, Maestro. A spell or two from a man of your profession and any lockpick would cringe in fear. Madonna mia, the tales I've heard—men turned to swine, fleas, even newts! No, signore, none would risk the wrath of an alchemist."

"If I thought I had the slightest chance of convincing you that I am not Circe, nor yet Hermes Trismegistus, I'd attempt it. Since I don't, I won't waste my breath. Just believe me when I tell you this is honest minted gold. You needn't fear it will turn to lead or dead leaves or some other superstitious nonsense."

Coffin opened his money chest and gave Angelo his fee. Angelo bit the coin, a conspirator's grin on his pointy face.

"Nice bit of work, if I do say so. It will pass anywhere in the city. You should be proud."

Coffin sighed. "Thank you, Angelo."

"Well, I'm off. Best part of the night ahead of me. Good luck with Handsome there," Angelo prattled as Coffin guided him to the door. "Oh, and my regards to your—"

Coffin froze him with a look.

"To, ah, your visitor, signore," Angelo finished lamely.

"Good night, Angelo." Coffin's voice was firm.

"So far," Angelo answered matter-of-factly, and vanished down the stair.

CHAPTER THREE

Nicholas leaned against the door, half expecting Angelo to return demanding more money for the cadaver. Before he pulled himself together to go to his workroom and begin the examination, another knock sounded at the door.

"Who is it?" he asked. If it was Angelo, he could just rest content with what he had been given.

"Temptation," came the reply, the voice invitingly husky. Nicholas opened the door, his long-jawed face breaking into a smile as he confronted his visitor.

She was fair, fair as any Englishwoman, and the honey of her hair matched the honey in her voice. The sophisticated gown she wore was purely Roman, as was the warmth of her dark eyes. With a slender hand, she flicked a gesture to the figure hulking behind her on the stair.

"Bring in my basket, Tranio," she said. "Thank you. That will be all for this evening."

Her servant rumbled a greeting to Coffin and brought in the basket with a silent grace his bulk belied, then bowed himself out, leaving her alone with the Englishman.

"Come in, Temptation, or whatever you will be tonight." Coffin beckoned her. "I take it Ludovico is out for the evening?"

"Oh, yes." She brushed past him and slipped her cloak off, handing it to Nicholas to hang beside his own. "He finally thought to send a message that he won't be home until morning. Good thing I was still there to receive it. He's at one of those arty suppers of his again, half noblemen and half prostitutes. They'll talk philosophy until the food is cold and then spend the rest of the evening discussing sex." She held out her hands to him palm up. "The nature of love, they call it."

"Disgraceful behavior," Nicholas assured her, taking her into his arms. He was as dark as she was fair, with a long-jawed face and rakish eyebrows that could only be English. He was tall by any standard; Costanza came only to his chin. She put her arms around him in turn and they stood breast to breast, silent. Abruptly, she shivered and drew more closely into the circle of his arms. "Poor Costanza," he said. "Would you like your cloak?"

"No, only hold me. I suppose you've had the windows open again, barbarous man."

"I'm sorry it seems cold to you, cara Costanza. In England—"

"Bother England. This isn't England. This is Rome and it would seem cold to anyone. It may snow tonight."

"It doesn't snow in Rome!"

"That's all you know of it, Englishman, for all you're always spouting history."

"But I've studied Rome—"

"And I've lived here all my life."

"But you didn't know about the Forum. If I hadn't told you, you'd still be speaking of it as if it were a marble quarry."

"When folk use it as such and the lime kilns burn the marble every day, I cannot be too ashamed of my wrong answer."

"That's their ignorance, and I find it typical of every Roman I've met."

"Still, they need the marble to make lime. Who needs a forum?"

"That requires a longer answer than you'll listen to tonight, little peach." Nicholas moved his hands from her shoulders to the nape of her neck, to stroke the fine short golden hairs there. Costanza arched her back luxuriously and purred, "Very right, Englishman. When I want lectures, I'll stay home with my husband."

"Harsh words from such tender lips," Nicholas mocked.

"In this world, I need to be harsh to get what I want. In another, better world, I will be meek and soft. And take no more lovers."

"You behave as though I were the first you'd taken—bringing baskets of food to your love—as though amorous thoughts trouble you even in the kitchen."

"Much more likely thoughts of waking up to no breakfast." Costanza assured him. "I know what

kind of ramshackle life you lead. It's only bread
and cheese. Believe me, it was a mere afterthought
when I learned I could stay all night."

Coffin watched her closely as she spoke and
pressed her no further, but he would have sworn
the blush on her cheek betrayed a vulnerability too
tender for jest. It was quite possible, he reflected,
that Costanza had known no one else—other than
her husband, of course. Their first night together
had given him a great desire to invite her previous
lover outside for a thorough beating, but after a
week of sleepless nights spent in each other's company, Nicholas had transformed Costanza from a
greedy lover expecting prodigies of fifteen minutes
duration and nothing thereafter, to a gentle and
complete lover who could idle a day and a night
away in the luxurious pleasantries of the bed. Her
greed sated by seven nights that gave Nicholas con-
siderable pleasure and an aching back, Costanza
had settled down to become the kind of lover that
looks alien with her clothes on—a kind of
Aphrodite, rising full born from seafoam and
bedsheets every night. If, as from her blush seemed
possible, she had had no lover before him but her
bookish husband, then there was the distinct possi-
bility that she was not simply adaptable, but genu-
inely unspoiled. Once freed from the monotonous
propriety of her husband's expectations, she had
displayed a taking ingenuity.

With that ingenuity in mind, he ran his fingers
from the nape of her neck to her shoulder blades,
then down to where the clasps of her gown began.

"Sweet Temptation," he began, "I know you do

not care for the common good, but have mercy on a simple man. That gown of yours is enough to madden a mob—the urge to take it off is unbearable."

"Easy to see from your anatomy—" Costanza pointed out. Nicholas glanced down at himself involuntarily.

"No," Costanza told him. "Your smile, as silly a smirk as any ram would wear."

Nicholas straightened his lean face.

"Mistress, I'd have use of you," he growled.

"Would you indeed?" Costanza asked dreamily. She turned and leaned against him so that her back pressed all along his front from knees and thighs up to shoulders and breast. Nicholas took a deep breath and savored her warmth, holding her close to him in an appreciative grasp. She sighed and leaned her weight along his strength, letting his hands loosen her gown.

"Gentle ram," she whispered, "use me as you would."

The fire along his veins quieted and gathered into a soft smolder, until his finger's ends traced fire across her skin and she lay before him on the bed, sighing for his touch.

Before the approaching dawn had done more than gray the eastern sky, there was a rising clamor in the Borgia apartments of the Vatican palace. One by one they came, the courtiers who were to have diced the night away, the servants who were to have drawn baths and laid out clothing. They came puzzled, expecting orders or explanations, but when they saw and spoke among themselves, their questions became gossip. Gossip became rumor and from rumor sprang alarm.

The Pope's valet surveyed the growing throng and realized he could delay no longer. Urged on by courtiers and servants, he led the way to the Pontiff's bedchamber and stood poised uncertainly for a moment outside the door, then, hesitation behind him, he tapped on the door panel, opened it and stepped inside.

Beneath the counterpane, quilted silk and swan's down against the January chill, the sleeping man's bulk was impressive, almost unhealthy. His slumber was punctuated by occasional grunting snorts, but none of his retinue would have dared to describe them as snores. Alexander VI had vices aplenty, but his servants knew better than to inform him of them if they could avoid it.

Humbly, the valet approached the bed and touched the Pope's nearest shoulder. With a stifled wheeze, Alexander snapped his eyes open and he sat up abruptly. The valet took an involuntary step backward.

Alexander glared, his dark eyes like raisins in his full, puffy face.

"I hope for your sake that this is important," he said, then let his eyes dart around the room, judging the faint light that peeped around the window shutters. "I was up until a few hours ago playing cards with Cesare."

"There are people without, your Holiness. They say your Holiness' son is missing. He was not seen yesterday. He never arrived at the Orsini banquet last night. There's been no sign of him at all—"

"My son?" Alexander repeated blankly. "Ercole? My little son?"

"Your Holiness," the valet choked, "they fear he has had some great—harm—befall him."

"Who fears?" Alexander demanded, throwing back the counterpane. He rose and drew on a robe, then moved for the door, resplendent in velvet and gold embroidery. "Who fears?"

In the apartment without, a dozen men who had gesticulated and whispered avidly a few moments before fell abruptly silent as the door was opened. Wide-eyed and speechless, they gazed terrified at the ox-shouldered man in the doorway.

"Who fears?" he said again, his eyes burning in his doughy face. "Who fears for our son?"

None spoke. A few shifted their eyes to the floor.

"Our son Ercole is safe, for no one would dare to harm him. Is he not our son?" Alexander paused, twitched his hawk nose and stared forbiddingly around the room. "Go now, and find him for us. Bring him here to his father and we will welcome him," he ordered.

The group of courtiers and serving men stirred.

"Well?" he roared. "Go!"

To a man, they made eagerly for the door, the valet among them. Alexander exhaled deeply and stepped back into his chamber alone, closed the door and stood with his hand on the latch. His little dark eyes widened, and he gazed blankly at the dimness of his room, and beyond. Then, the corners of his wide mouth tightened and his eyes focused again, this time on the elaborate little altar in the corner of the room and the exquisite ivory crucifix above it.

"Another son?" he whispered, regarding the twisted ivory figure on the cross. "Must you take from me another son?"

Heavily, he walked to the altar and knelt down before it. But though he knelt there unmoving, the silence in the room was unbroken either by prayer or curse.

When Nicholas awoke, the room was still dark, but the blackness was fading so that he could make out shapes in the gloom—the chair with their clothes draped upon it, the little table strewn with Costanza's jeweled hairpins. He stretched and felt Costanza's warmth stir beside him. Unwillingly, he recalled the cold presence awaiting him in his workroom. Curiosity lashed at him like a scourge and drove sleepiness away. He swung his legs over the edge of the narrow bed and slumped there for a moment, rubbing his face wearily.

"Morning so soon?" Costanza asked, her voice low and husky with sleep. She raised herself on one elbow and peered about her, then let the blanket fall from her shoulders to push her blonde hair out of her eyes.

Nicholas regarded her for a moment, then looked around in the dimness.

"No," he decided, "my mistake." He pulled his long legs back under the blankets and reached for her. She put her hand against his chest and held him away for a moment.

"There is no hurry, Niccolo, whatever the time," she reminded him.

"I pity poor Ludo, wrestling the night away with philosophy."

"At least they pay him," she yawned. "He should pay them to listen."

"Beautiful cynic," Nicholas scolded. "What is knowledge to you that you should mock your learned husband?"

"*Zut!* Knowledge, learning—it's tiresome." Costanza ran her warm fingers from his chest into the darkness between his thighs. "Still," she purred, "I am learned too, in some things."

"And those things," Nicholas murmured, half to himself, "are not at all tiresome."

Across the city, as the day ripened, a fat man crouched before an altar in his private chambers. The silence in the room had grown deep and taken on a character of its own. His face set, his hands clenched, the man's thoughts were not on his younger son, but on his elder.

With the cruel clarity only unpleasant memories possess, his thoughts ranged back, not to the night before with its jesting card game, but to the preceding evening.

The January sunlight had faded into the rich indigo of twilight when he joined his sons. They had been dicing amiably and Ercole had just lost the gold pin and egret cockade he wore in his velvet cap. They rose at his entrance, their long-limbed grace a comfort to the eye. He beamed with fierce pride upon their litheness, their youth. Who would not be proud to sire such tall boys as these: Cesare, auburn-haired and magnificent, Ercole, slender and blond, black-clad in open imitation of his elder brother.

"So," he greeted them, "you come to dine with me?"

Ercole flicked an imaginary speck of lint from his immaculate velvet sleeve and smiled his tomcat smile.

"My apologies, father," he said, "but I am engaged for the evening and must leave shortly. It's not the sort of entertainment I'd care to be late for."

"More tutoring for the Orsini speech, doubtless," Cesare judged with a knowing smile.

"And you?" he asked his elder son.

"Not tonight," he said, his voice cool. His face was an expressionless mask, bland and debonair. "Tonight I have business. Tomorrow we will all dine together while Ercole impresses the Orsini, and we will enjoy ourselves, whatever the Orsini do. But this evening, I have business."

So he had dined alone, when his tall sons had left him, and thought nothing more about it. Then, the next evening, Ercole had not joined them at dinner and Cesare had lied for him to blunt the caustic words of the Orsini lordlings. They had made a short evening of the great occasion and gone home to play at cards together, but though Cesare was very witty and gay, he had said nothing of his business of the night before. He had given no hint of where he had been, nor any clue to what he had done. It had not seemed strange then, but now, in the thin light of morning, the kneeling Father asked himself where his son had been. Where had he been and what could he have done?

CHAPTER FOUR

Later that morning, Coffin stood across the street from the house Costanza's husband owned, and watched her open windows. He had escorted her home before full daylight. Customarily, Costanza depended on Tranio to protect her from the Roman streets, but on this occasion, his absence had forced them to risk being seen together in the street. Short as their time together had seemed, Costanza had arrived home only a perilously short period of time before Ludovico himself. Now, while Ludovico undoubtedly demanded his breakfast, Costanza was directing the flurry of her household's morning routine. The routine of opening windows was an imprompt one, begun because Costanza, despite her dislike of cold air, had discovered that she could smile out the window at Nicholas while she conversed meekly with her husband, all under the guise of housewifery. Also, Nicholas strongly suspected, Costanza's distaste for the cold amounted to nothing beside Ludovico's.

Even while he smiled at Costanza, Coffin's mind turned to the other caller he had received the night before.

With luck, he told himself, there should be no difficulty about the body if he finished examining it in time to dispose of it after dark. No one would be missed in that short a time. A nobleman of the station indicated by the corpse's clothing could vanish for far more than twenty-four hours before he would be considered missing. The fleshpots of Rome held charms that could make a man desert his friends for much longer than a few days and nights.

Bringing his mind back to Costanza, Coffin realized that he had been smiling for some minutes at an empty window. Evidently household routine had taken the happy couple elsewhere in the house. With a shrug, Coffin turned for home and began threading his way absently through alleys and backstreets, his mind on Angelo's prize.

In his experience with cadavers, he had never seen one with characteristics as charmingly peculiar as this one. Reviewing the alluring symptoms the body displayed, he did not at first notice his landlady as he reached his quarters and started up the stair, but once she stepped out into his path to sweep the steps before him, he could hardly ignore her.

"Morning," she grunted, bending over her broom with uncharacteristic zeal. "Have a nice night?"

Coffin surveyed her slowly from thickened ankles to dishevelled, stringy hair and curled his lip to show his disfavor. He did not for a moment suppose that she had any genuine interest in his answer.

"To tell you the truth, Bianca," he drawled, "I hardly got a wink of sleep."

"Oh? Too bad, then. Heard the news?"

"I imagine I will if I wait a moment."

"Pope's bastard is gone. They don't know if he got it into his head to leave the city, or if somebody did away with him. Just like a few years back when they found the older son, that Juan, floating face down in the Tevere. Well, no mystery who did that. His little brother Cesare didn't look sad long. And now the youngest one is gone. They're searching the river. History repeats itself, eh?"

Coffin let the spate of chatter run over him, hoping she would either get to the point or lose interest and leave him alone. When she paused, he opened his eyes hopefully, but it was evident from the eager gleam in her eye she was only waiting for some commonplace from him to continue.

"Bad luck to be Cesare Borgia's brother, it seems," he said, reluctantly.

"Yes, that one's bad, bold and bad. They noticed the young one was gone last night. He was supposed to blow hard with some speech at the Orsini palazzo to show what a scholar he is."

"He was probably warm in bed somewhere."

"While his papa the Pope blushes in front of the Orsini? Tell me another. Not that the old bull knows how to blush, any more than any other Borgia."

"Out late one night and he's cold meat? Ercole Borgia? All the Borgias have nine lives, like cats," Coffin retorted.

"Well, if he's alive, he'll wish he weren't when his family finds him. He made them look silly and they're turning Rome upside down looking for him."

"More likely he'll stay with whatever kitten he's found until they're all glad to welcome him back from the dead."

"A ducat says he is dead," Bianca offered hopefully.

Coffin suddenly realized the stupidity of the argument he had been engaged in and shook himself angrily. "You have a ducat to spare?" he asked.

"I'll take it off your rent."

"Sorry. If I meet anyone who hasn't heard the news, I'll send them to you and you can gamble with them."

"You're a cold fish, Englishman," Bianca informed him, and stopped all pretense of sweeping the stair. With a sniff of disdain, she went back down to the door, broom on her sloping shoulder.

"Nice try," called Coffin after her.

"I'd have given you two to one odds if you'd not have given up so easy."

"Next time, Bianca," he promised, and went to his quarters.

Once inside, Nicholas closed the door and locked it. With long strides, he entered his workroom and closed that door firmly, then walked to the work table where his uninvited guest lay. Eyes wide with apprehension, he reached out and turned back one of the black velvet cuffs to reveal the shirt beneath the doublet. The fabric was still damp but the delicate embroidery was clearcut Spanish blackwork, a running fretwork of black threads in which bulls charged and roses blossomed. Thoughtfully, he fingered the fabric. The bull was the badge of the Pope's family, and there was no family deadlier than that of Alexander VI, he who had once been known as Roderigo Borgia.

Coffin lifted his eyes to the cadaver and spoke in a husky, wrathful whisper, "You had a ring or two with the badge too, I suppose, before Angelo stole them. If I'd thought to look last night, I could have seen Borgia written all over you—and your shirt. By God, it was probably your own brother or sister who killed you, with some cheating little poisoned cup of milk. I'm surprised you only turned blue. You could have come out in carbuncles with a family like yours dosing you. Christ, your father's the Pope. He could have summoned up a miracle and turned you into loaves and fishes. But no, you turn blue. And what miserable timing! Any other night and you could have been killed with impunity but last night you had an invitation from the Orsini. You wretched bastard."

Coffin paced the length of the room in silence, turned on his heel and paced back.

"I wish you were alive so I could kill you again," he rasped. "But I don't care who you are, you're blue and I intend to find out why."

With speed and dispatch, he stripped the corpse and tossed the garments into a corner and laid out the cadaver. Then, with the charcoal pellets that cost him too many carlini to waste, he fired up the athanor and opened the window to let the poisonous fumes escape into the chill outside air. While the furnace heated, he assembled his most complex piece of apparatus, essentially a tiny still comprised of the round curcurbit base over the heat source, the goose-necked alembic atop it, and the nearly spherical aludel receiver that the alembic's "beak" fed into. The aludel, given to him by his sometime teacher, Flamel, was not of the usual baked clay strengthened with horsehair, but of the clearest handblown glass. He buffed it on his doublet sleeve, then put it into place, ready to receive the condensed distillate the alembic would produce. Then, he deftly set out his array of flasks and vials ready for use. Finally, he poured fresh water into a basin, rolled up his sleeves, and washed carefully. He dried his hands on a clean towel and tucked its edge into his belt, available to clean his hands as he worked.

Three hours later, the towel was soaked scarlet. Coffin pulled it from his belt and dropped it in a corner. The dead man's torso was an unrecognizabel array of components, though his face was still a tranquil mask regarding the ceiling. Nicholas turned from the body without letting his concentration falter. Without a thought, he stripped off his sweaty doublet and shirt and poured more water into the basin to splash over his flushed face and neck.

Back at the table, he slid his finely honed scalpel between the layers of tissue in the stomach and spread the opening with a practiced touch. The cavity's contents were partially digested, but not plentiful.

"You either had a very light meal, or something you ate disagreed with you rather violently. Either way, you don't seem to have enjoyed your last supper."

He transferred the half-digested food deftly to a glass container and set it aside.

"You didn't drink much water, from the look of things. Did you have a chance to breathe any?" he inquired mildly, all the while probing into the lungs with his gleaming blade. "Come on, let's have it. You don't have gills. Admit it. You were dead for quite some time before you hit the water. You haven't a bruise or garotte mark anywhere about you, nor any slice marks but what I've put on you. Deepest apologies and all that, but the first cut was Angelo's. I'm just rummaging about trying to make very sure you died the way any man in his right mind would assume you died, you being who you are. You might say that he who lives by the poison shall die by the poison. You blue devil, you. You're red enough inside, though. Let's have a bit of this kidney to match what's on the fire now, shall we?" Coffin transferred the tissue to its glass receptacle. "Angelo didn't get much blood out of you when he took your rings. No, it looks like it's going to be the obvious conclusion."

He put his scalpel down with a precise click and went to inspect the athanor and its contents. He added more charcoal and went to the window to lean out into the welcome chill. Coffin looked down into the garden and eyed the marble hand with its marble grapes below.

"Never a corpse in England with the temerity to turn blue. Nor ever the peace to work on a cadaver in private, either. I wonder what Flamel would make of this." He turned back to the corpse and took up the scalpel again, feeling with steady fingers for the intestines where they lay under the smooth blue skin. "Perhaps I'll ask him. He likes poison."

By the time he was done, the sunlight was gone and the athanor's warmth was losing its battle with the chill of winter. A dozen glass flasks were lined up beside the athanor, each neatly filled with samples of the dead man's anatomy. Inside the little furnace six earthenware crucibles glowed red, and above, the alembic still bubbled.

"Your soul may possibly have gone to heaven, Borgia, but your body will never know. Part of it, anyway. I suppose the rest of you is cold enough to offset the heat in here."

Coffin began the unpleasant business of re-assembling and stitching the remnants, ignoring the chill and gathering darkness. Finally, he rolled the cadaver into his oldest blanket and sewed it into a shroud.

"Now," he murmured, we wait. When it's full dark, and not before, you'll get buried where no one's going to find you and be inspired to search for the man who took you apart. It will be a nuisance, mind you, and if you cause the least disturbance, it's back to the river with you and damn the risk. As for Flamel, though I know he'd enjoy meeting you, I think he'll have to make do with the bits you've left behind. Or my description of them. I know you've left your heart here, but I promise I'll take you somewhere very peaceful to make up for it. So as I said, now we wait."

CHAPTER FIVE

Down in the narrow street, the gloom was deep, moonlight shut out by the looming buildings. A wind whistled out of the north down into the alleys, making it difficult to hear the rustle of an oncoming intruder. Coffin shouldered his burden and walked briskly from the steps of Bianca's house to the nearest alley. It was sixty steps and by the time he reached the shelter of the alley mouth he was breathing rapidly. He put the bundle down and waited a moment, straining to hear over the breeze. No sound came to him down the wind. He lifted the bulk again and writhed it into place over his shoulders. His soft boots moved slowly, searching for firm footing on the rough paving of the alley. Once he sank ankle deep in mud, righted himself, and clenched his jaw to keep from cursing aloud.

As he continued on, slow but silent, he felt sweat trickle down his spine, chilled by the fitful night wind. The muscles between his shoulder blades tightened. It was not wise to be out at this hour burdened with a dead weight that could hamper his self defense. Even as the thought came to him the wind dropped and he heard a boot-scrape from the darkness before him, menacing in its softness.

Coffin felt every muscle tense into readiness. A gleam of light lanced out from a shielded lantern, dazzling his eyes. A voice spoke from behind the light.

"Oh, Maestro Coffin—didn't expect to see you out this time of night. Sorry." The deep voice of the speaker had the accent of the Trastevere slums.

"Wait a minute," a second, harsher voice spoke up. "What's going on? We're supposed to rob him."

"I know that, blockhead. I've been at this longer than you. But you don't go robbing friends," the first voice retorted. "At least, not this friend. He'll turn you on your head before you get a hand on his purse."

Coffin's eyes were well enough adjusted to the lantern light by now to recognize the first speaker as Aldo, a thug he occasionally saw in wineshops across the river. The other voice belonged to a huskier man with a scar running from the outer corner of his left eye down to his chin. Scarface did not appear willing to change his plans for any friend of Aldo's.

"Good evening," Coffin greeted Aldo. "I haven't seen you down at the Silver Snail lately."

"You know how it is," Aldo replied. "Cold weather's bad for business. I don't have the profits I used to."

"No talk," Scarface grated. "Put that bundle down and let's see your money."

"Well, go ahead," Aldo said. "I warned you."

"What's to be afraid of?" Scarface demanded. "He's a foreigner, so what?"

"There are foreigners and foreigners. Flamel knows him."

Scarface paused momentarily, and Coffin took his hesitation as a cue to pounce forward. He dropped his chin and let the cadaver sail over his head toward Scarface.

Aldo had taken a prudent step backward, so Scarface took the full brunt of the body's weight. He fell backward, boot heels slipping in the oily mud. Coffin followed the cadaver and went down on top of the thief, knees and elbows first. A knife flashed in the lantern light. Coffin caught the wrist that held it and stopped the blow inches from his face. His knee jabbed a vulnerable spot as he gave the wrist a vicious twist. Something in the joint snapped and Scarface screamed. Coffin snatched the knife away and held the edge to the thug's throat.

"Keep your mouth shut or I'll cut you another one right here," Coffin rasped savagely. Scarface's eyes bulged and he held his breath at the prick of the knife.

Aldo leaned close with the lantern to chide his partner.

"Now, see? I warned you. Let him up, Maestro. He knows better now. You'll be good, won't you?"

The fallen man rolled his eyes and whispered, "Yes, signore. I will."

Coffin rose in a single fluid motion and pocketed the knife.

"Keep the babies in at night, why don't you?" he asked. "The streets aren't safe for them at this hour."

"You're absolutely right, Maestro," Aldo nodded. "Sorry to be a trouble. Have a nice stroll."

"Good night for it," Coffin replied, and waited where he was while Scarface was helped up and away. Only when his protests had faded on the wind did Coffin take up his bundle once again.

Fortunately, at the next corner he found what he sought. A woodseller's cart, left by its owner for a late bicker with a customer, stood unattended in the street. Coffin deposited his burden in the cart and judiciously arranged kindling to conceal it. He calmly picked up the shafts of the cart and took it away with him into the shadows, leaving the owner and customer locked in debate.

His progress through the backstreets was uneventful. He paused only to sell a half dozen sticks of kindling to an old woman with a wen. After an hour of steering the cart between potholes, he pulled it up next to a dark doorway smelling of urine.

His knock at the door went unanswered for so long Coffin feared he had come too late. At last, the latch lifted and a voice growled, "What's your business here?"

Coffin leaned down to meet the speaker's eye. She was a crone of great age and greater filth, with a smell of wet straw clinging to her.

"I'm here to see Basilio," he said, leaning close to let her see his face.

"Well, Englishman," she purred unwholesomely. "Good thing you came no later. He's getting ready to go to work."

"Maybe I'll go along and talk," Coffin offered.

"You can go along," her voice cracked into a chuckle, "But you won't get much talking done. It's not talking work."

"What are you gassing about, woman?" Basilio's voice rumbled from the dark behind her. "Out of the way, will you? My arms are full."

From the void behind the door came a scrape of stone on wood and a stifled curse. Then Basilio was out on the threshold, balancing a loosely wrapped parcel in his arms.

"Put that in my cart and let me share your walk to work," Coffin suggested.

"Ho, Nicholas!" Basilio greeted him softly. "Thought I heard your voice. Here, I'll take you up on that. Steady—"

With a subdued crash, Basilio placed his burden in the woodcart and stretched his heavily muscled arms. "Jesu Maria, I like to have ruptured myself with that. Stupid line of work. Here, wait a bit and let me get my shovel. I'm late already." He smoothed one hand over his dark close-cropped hair from crown to nape, as though stroking an animal's pelt. "Lucky you happened along, eh?" he remarked, and shot Nicholas a sharp look before he vanished within.

In a moment he emerged with his tools on his

shoulder. He dropped them unceremoniously into the cart and helped Coffin maneuver the wheels into the well-worn ruts in the street.

"So," Basilio said at last, "what brings you along at this hour?"

"Nice night for a stroll, I thought," Coffin replied, thinking of Aldo. "Do you usually take so much luggage to work?"

"Oh, that—" Basilio prodded his bundle with a forefinger. "That's a special job. Some antique dealer wants me to bury it outside the walls. It's a statue. Some friend of his carved it and sold it to him. The dealer got the idea to knock its arm off and bury it, then dig it up and say it's an antique. That will triple the price it will bring."

"Heavy work for you, though."

"It pays." Basilio stroked his head again. "I can always get a corpse on the way back from the cemetery and make an easy few soldi selling it to some painter who wants to cut it up on the sly and draw all the muscles."

Coffin nodded and went on silently pulling at the woodcart. Basilio pulled along beside him for a dozen strides, then cleared his throat.

"Lucky you came by tonight," he said at last.

Coffin nodded again but did not answer.

"I never knew you to sell wood before," Basilio persisted.

"Basilio," Coffin began, then paused.

"Yes?"

"I'd like to borrow your shovel, once we get to the cemetery."

Basilio's eyebrows rose and his hand automatically went up to stroke his hair from crown to nape. He stole a look back at the cart and its contents.

"Sure, Englishman," he said finally. "Whatever you say."

CHAPTER SIX

Just after sundown on the following evening Coffin made his way from wineshop to wineshop, keeping his eyes open for familiar faces— Scarface's among them. He had been back in his quarters before sunrise, to spend the day abed. Once his lost sleep had been made up, and he had restored himself with the last remnants of Costanza's basket, he had dressed and gone in search of information. It was dressing that had made him wish to encounter Scarface again. Rolling in the alley mud had ruined his warmest suit of clothing and the jerkin he had chosen as second choice had sleeves just too short for comfort. They made him edgy, and he wished he had Scarface's wrist back to twist a little harder.

The thug never did appear, but in the third tavern on his route, Coffin found someone he was even more pleased to see.

"Angelo!"

The little man was alone at a corner table, slumped over a winecup. At the sound of Coffin's voice he sat upright and gazed wildly about the room. Without meeting Coffin's eyes he slid back down into his seat on the bench and attempted to slither past the alchemist toward the door. Coffin caught him by the collar and put him gently back on the bench, sliding in to sit beside him and keep him pinned in the corner. The buzz of the tavern crowd went on, oblivious of them.

"Hello, Angelo. How are you these days?" Coffin inquired affably.

"Please," Angelo whispered, straining to look at the Englishman out of the corners of his eyes. He held his head rigidly still and appeared to be gazing fixedly at the door. "Not so loud."

"Oh, I'm fine," Coffin went on, ignoring Angelo's facial contortions. "I'm glad to hear you've been so well employed since I saw you last."

"For the love of heaven, Maestro," Angelo turned to him with an expression of horror. "Keep your voice down. One word too many—we're dead men."

"So you've guessed too," Coffin said more softly.

Angelo nodded tightly and gulped at his wine.

"What luck," he said gloomily.

"Is that what's to blame?" Coffin's voice was cold. "Luck?"

"Honest," Angelo pleaded. "You've got to believe me, Maestro. I didn't know!"

Coffin stared at Angelo icily for a moment longer, then relented and said, "Yes, I believe you."

Angelo jumped, slopping wine out of his cup. "You do? Why?"

"Because you stole his rings. If you'd known what we had, you'd have known that any one of that man's rings was as good as a death sentence."

Angelo's eyes widened but he did not speak. Coffin caught the barmaid's eye and waved her over to order more wine. Angelo refilled his winecup and stared into it moodily.

"But, Maestro, what shall we do?"

Coffin took a large swallow of wine and fixed Angelo with his dark gaze.

"We shall catch the killer. It's the only way to avoid the inevitable when the family catches us."

"Catch the—" Angelo choked.

"The killer. Whoever slipped a dose into little Ercole's supper."

"A dose? He was poisoned?"

"He didn't die of old age." Coffin refilled his winecup.

"What kind of poison?" Angelo asked.

"That, I can't be precise about." The alchemist's eyes narrowed. "At first I thought of arsenic, or antimony. But it's neither of those. The only traces I can find that could be toxic look almost like a dye."

"A dye?" Comprehension dawned in Angelo's eyes. "Blue dye?"

"No. Green dye," Coffin responded absently. Then both his brows rose and he glared at Angelo.

"Really, Angelo, the problem's not that simple. You think he was blue because someone dyed him blue? Don't be naive."

"But who would put green dye in his dinner? And who wouldn't notice if someone did?" Angelo asked.

"That's not an unreasonable question." Coffin leaned closer. "Next to my landlady, you know more gossip than anyone alive in Rome today. I want you to put your pointed donkey ears to the ground and start collecting rumors."

"What kind of rumors?"

"When was Ercole seen last, who was with him, what courtesan was he sleeping with, who hates him most—that kind of thing."

"Everybody knows those things," Angelo replied. "He was supposed to see his mistress the night before they missed him at the Orsini palazzo. He was seen on his way there and not since. He sleeps with the mistress, mostly. Nobody hated him, except maybe his brother Cesare."

"Ah, yes. The lethal Cesare." Coffin's eyes narrowed.

"You'd better watch out, Maestro. Ever since his brother has been missing, he's had his men out on the streets watching."

"Watching for what?"

"Anything. Any trace of Ercole. Anything suspicious at all. Last night they picked up a man in Trastevere."

Coffin felt a shiver slide up his back. "What for?"

"Nothing. He had a cloak on that was the same color as Ercole's. They questioned him and let him go, but they're still looking. We'd better be careful."

"Cesare Borgia doesn't own this town yet," Coffin replied.

"You'd be surprised," Angelo told him. "You've only been here a year. You don't know Rome as well as you think."

"They can't watch everywhere. We'll just have to be careful. Keep your eyes open. Just give me the name of Ercole's mistress. I'll take care of her."

"You will? She's Giulietta," the little man said dubiously.

"*The* Giulietta?" Coffin raised an eyebrow.

"The one and only." Angelo drained his winecup.

Coffin stared at Angelo absently. Giulietta, called La Bella Bellissima, the fairest fair, was the choicest, if not precisely the freshest, of Rome's courtesans. From the usual graceless past, she had found her way into the first and most fashionable circles, until now she held one of the most envied places in Roman society. She was a woman so fascinating and of such varied talents that she no longer needed to heed the tenets of fashion. She had purchased an elegant villa and was allowing a succession of admirers to fill it with what jewels, clothing, and art works suited her best. Her taste was impeccable and her instinct for survival bordered on genius.

"He would have been a little young for her, certainly?"

"These last few months she's collected lovers the way she collects paintings," Angelo answered. "Goes through them like a hot knife through butter. There's no telling who'll be next. Noblemen, scholars—she even had a painter for awhile."

"She should be interesting to visit."

"If you get as far as her garbage in the gutter outside, I'll be surprised. She doesn't like strangers," Angelo warned.

"We'll see." Coffin finished his wine. "We'll see."

"I'm sure we will," said Angelo glumly.

CHAPTER SEVEN

After the lamp glow of the wineshop, Coffin's eyes adjusted slowly to the gloom outside. His initial search in the first two taverns had taken more time than he had thought, for as he stepped from the noisy warmth of the wineshop into the dark, he heard the first strokes of the church bells throughout the city tolling midnight.

The chill of the night air was a shock and he tucked his fingers under his arms for warmth. Without warning, a blow lanced out of the blackness, grazing his head and landing with force intact on his right shoulder. Pain flashed through him like white light. He rolled with the blow by instinct, trying to get his balance, but a second blow came, and then a third. The world shut down into darkness and the tolling of bells. A fourth blow fell and darkness swallowed darkness.

Sound came back first, and a sense of warmth.

Slowly, he gathered his senses, analyzed what they told him. He could hear the crackle of a fire and feel warmth on his face. There was a smell of wood smoke and perfume. The scent was expensive, chypre, he judged, worth a gold piece a dram. The street fighter in him overruled the alchemist and he ran a quick check of his aches. Right shoulder: sore but not broken. Skull: dented and aching but no more damage done. None, at least, that he could discern from within. Judging himself intact and ready to handle those who had mishandled him so, he opened his eyes.

The room was dimly lit and as expensive as the scent. Small bronze statuettes ornamented the mantel of the yawning fireplace that provided light as well as heat. Across from the chair where Coffin found himself, a man stood against the mantelpiece, idly watching the flames lick about the logs.

His first glimpse of the man, through headache fog and firelight, made Coffin think of a lion. He was tall, taller even than Coffin, and held himself as regally as a king. His costume was rich and somber, his hair dark red, cut in a mane to his broad shoulders. The shoulders' width disguised the inordinate size of the man's head, but as he turned to look at Coffin, a heaviness about his gaze and the disproportionate size of his head made his likeness to a lion more striking.

In the firelight, his eyes were golden.

Abruptly, transfixed by the man's gaze, Coffin felt a great awareness of his shabby clothing, badly cut sleeves, and slumping posture in the richly carved chair. He felt smaller and dirtier than he was used to feeling. Then, although the gaze never faltered, anger burnt self-consciousness away. He forcibly kept himself from straightening up and only lounged more languidly in the chair.

Like a great cat, the golden-eyed man stalked elegantly from the fire to loom over him.

"Who," he asked in a deep velvety voice, "are you?"

Coffin stretched his long legs out to the fire's warmth. "I am Nicholas Coffin, master of arts. I am a subject of the English crown. Do you often solicit guests this way?"

"Never guests," the tall man replied. In response to Coffin's frank stare he said, "I am Cesare Borgia."

"I suspected as much." Coffin rose stiffly from his chair. "How may I serve you, my lord?"

"Please dispense with formality, sir," Borgia answered. "I have had occasion to watch you before you woke, and you surprise me, I admit."

"I do?" Coffin's dark eyes met Borgia's golden ones, startled.

"Indeed." Borgia lounged his way back to the fireplace and held out his hands to it, basking in the warmth. "Indeed you do, sir. You have a trifling accent, to be sure, but still better than most foreigners. Your clothing is deplorable, but your demeanor is not altogether hopeless. No, not at all what I expected of a thievish body-snatcher from the streets." Borgia's final words lashed coldly, but

Coffin relaxed visibly at his change in tone.

"You mystify me, your Eminence," he said calmly.

"Oh, dispense with that title. I have, some while since." Borgia's tone was once more one of boredom.

"I am a scholar, not a thief. My studies have taken me down strange avenues, I admit, but I am no ghoul," Coffin protested.

"No? Yet you study dead men."

"They can be most informative."

Coffin's words hung in the air for a long moment. When Borgia spoke presently it was as though he had forgotten what had gone before.

"You have not asked me why you are here," he said.

Coffin said nothing, only looked around him at the dim splendor of the room.

Borgia watched his gaze move from the antique figurines to the frescoed wall panels.

"No," he said, amused by Coffin's expression, "not the trappings of a cell. Yet you are in a stronghold, Englishman. I built it myself, here in Trastevere. The poor folk of Trastevere love and admire me, Englishman. Don't ask me why. Perhaps because I do what they would if they were in a high position and not a low one. Who can say? Still, here you are and here you will remain. My younger brother was very dear to my father. So dear, in fact, he is questioning himself in the matter of how dear he was to me. Such doubts must not be allowed to trouble him. His mind must be put at ease."

"It must grieve your father to lose another child. Your elder brother died not many years ago, did he not?"

"My brother Juan kept rough company. For a man with as little acumen as he possessed, it is not astounding he met the end he did." Borgia's tone was stern.

"Even the Pope must accept the will of God," Coffin observed piously. "Forgive my tactlessness. All this occurred before I ever came to Rome."

Borgia turned a withering gaze on Coffin. "Your apology is accepted. Any lingering offense could be atoned for by telling me what you know of my brother Ercole."

"I? I only know what all Rome knows—"

"Spare me your pathetic dissimulations. Where is my brother?"

"I was about to say, all Rome knows of your intelligence system. When your spies and informants cannot help you, how can I?"

"My men have helped me. They brought you to me. Did you not wonder how my excellent system of spies and informants located you so efficiently? Last night a common street robber with a broken wrist earned fifty carlini for telling one of my men about a 'Maestro Coffin' who was out for a stroll with a dead body sewn into a blanket. Coffin is unmistakably an English name. It was a simple matter to ascertain your whereabouts through the English ambassador, as your family sends you letters of credit from time to time. Income from your inheritance, I believe the ambassador said. It astonishes me you have such a background, but I believe the English are famous for their mongrel families. Still, the important matter is that you were found. Does it please you to know your worth? Fifty carlini."

Coffin rose to meet the nobleman's gaze directly. Eyes locked, the two men stood before the hearth. The firelight threw both faces into sharp relief. Something in the set of Coffin's broad shoulders must have betrayed his street fighting aptitude, for the taller man drew back slightly and said with a trace of surprise, "You don't look like a scholar, Englishman."

When he finally spoke, Coffin's voice was deceptively soft. "But I am."

"Suppose, only suppose," Borgia's voice held a slight hesitation, "that a scholar of such things had an opportunity to examine a dead man. No particular dead man, of course, and the opportunity would arise through purest accident alone. What could that examination tell a scholar?"

"Most scholars?" Coffin replied cautiously, "That dead men grow cold with time. Any *one* such scholar, should he be assured that this examination would not come to the attention of the law that would surely execute him for studying the dead?" Coffin lifted an eyebrow and waited.

"Yes, yes," Borgia nodded eagerly. "Forget the law. What could 'any *one* such' scholar tell me?"

"He could tell you within a few hours when the man died. He could tell you when the dead man's final meal was, whether he drowned or had his head crushed in, if he drank himself to death or was run over by a horse, or if he ate oysters out of season."

Borgia leaned forward slightly. "And if this same scholar had examined my brother?"

"If he were rash enough to admit it to his captor while he was a prisoner, he could tell him the youth was poisoned."

"Why rash?" Borgia seemed taken aback.

"Though he can tell how, how can he say who? The scholar loves the truth. He would like to learn who the poisoner was and get evidence to prove it."

"Do you fear to do that?"

"It depends on whether the captor wants his scholar to prove who the poisoner was."

Borgia stiffened and took a step back.

"Do you presume to accuse me?"

"By no means. I'll admit, however, your response heartens me."

Borgia bent forward as though to gather all Coffin's attention into those golden eyes.

"If I had done what you imply, I would not be searching every alley in Rome for the man who killed my brother."

"Not even to keep suspicion from falling on you?"

Borgia stiffened as if he were about to pounce.

"I am above suspicion," he said.

Coffin shrugged easily and said nothing.

Borgia spun on his heel and stalked away from the fireplace. After a moment came a hiss as he expelled a hard-held breath of self-control. In the dimness, Coffin saw his hand reach out, dwarfing a costly figurine. He hefted it, as if to hurl it from him, then set it back with a precise click. Drawing in another deep breath, he stalked back to the hearth. His head was held low as he walked and his eyes burned golden from under his brows. His voice tight, he regarded Coffin levelly. "You say it was poison. I have the resources to make you tell me all the rest you know."

"I know."

Eyes ablaze, Borgia raised a clenched fist and held it under Coffin's nose. It was rock steady.

"You don't seem to realize it," Borgia said, "but I am the most dangerous man in Rome."

"I know."

"Then what makes you stand there facing me? I could have you untied sinew by sinew. What do you have for a defense against me?" he demanded. "Wealth? Influence? Some secret to sell?"

"Knowledge," Coffin answered quietly. Before the angry man could reply, he continued. "I have studied for years to master languages and learning lost in the drift of centuries. Aristotle, Galen—they could have told you. Your brother was poisoned and I know it. I can discover who was responsible and prove it, too. I have the knowledge, if only you will set it to work. I can clear your family of any breath of suspicion. How can your honor let this go unavenged? I can bring you the killer and proof of the crime. Only I have the skill to judge what the poison was and how it was administered."

"I could accuse you and wring your confession

out on the rack. My brother's death would be avenged beyond question."

"And the true culprit would still run free. Is that vengeance?"

For a moment, as Borgia's mouth twisted, Coffin thought he had stepped too far, but the tall man mastered himself and tossed his head. The mane of auburn hair rippled.

"You puzzle me, Englishman," he said. "You are nothing, a poor scholar, a puffing alchemist hunched in a roomful of smoke. I know your kind. Your clothes are dirty and your shirt needs mending. You have a mistress who is married to someone else because you can't afford to keep her, let alone a wife. You probably cheat at cards. Why should I believe you? Why should I listen to you? Yet somehow you've managed to push me closer to losing my temper than I've been this past year. Even such a dubious skill must have a use." He laughed softly. "It is a great temptation to set you loose. Oh, yes. A gadfly to bite where you will. I think you would not stick at stinging anyone as you have been stinging me." He chuckled again, his fists unclenched at last. "Go, then," he said, golden eyes aglow. "Accuse whom you will. Do as you please. But—" his eyes went icy, "my brother's funeral is in two days' time. Have this culprit brought to me by then or you'll pay the forfeit. Depend upon it."

"The funeral?"

"My men found his body this evening before they brought you here. They are very thorough."

For the first time in their interview, Coffin could not find words. He realized his jaw had dropped and closed it hastily.

Borgia tilted his head back and laughed coldly.

"Go now, Englishman. Question and insult as you have questioned and insulted me. Do what you will. Only remember, you have until my brother's funeral. Do not try to flee. As you know, I have my followers. Let me put it this way—from the moment you leave my house, you will have followers too. You would not get an hour's ride closer to your England. Stay in Rome and be a gadfly, scholar."

Coffin gathered himself and made a courtier's bow.

"I am at your command, my lord."

"Yes," Borgia nodded easily, "you are. Good hunting."

CHAPTER EIGHT

The corridor outside Borgia's chamber was already lightened with the gray dawn and stirring with the bustle of servitors. Just beyond the door a painter's scaffold barred the way. Borgia slid past it with a tiger's grace and smiled up at the painter.

"So ambitious, Lorenzo?"

The artist started and dropped a dollop of yellow ochre off the tip of his brush. He looked up from the spatter to say softly, "Your grace, I did not hear your approach."

"I was chiding you, bumpkin. These are not city ways, to come to work at dawn. A fashionable artist will yawn in at midday and scold his apprentice until the light is gone."

"Then I am not fashionable, your grace." The fair-skinned youth flushed painfully.

"No," Borgia agreed, enjoying the moment. He had a look of relish at the boy's discomfiture and at the inconvenience to which he had put his staff, blocking the way to his chamber while he paused to tease the painter. Coffin eyed Borgia's gloating warily, readying himself should the nobleman's mood change, and his decision with it.

"No," Borgia said again. "But you will be. So meantime, spare your eyes and come in later in the day when you can see to paint. I did not choose you from the herd to lose you to your bumpkinly ambitions."

The servants tittered appreciatively and Borgia strolled on, leaving the curly-haired youth with his teeth gritted into a smile at his master's wit.

"Hear that?" a valet crowed, nudging the artist's leg through the scaffolding. "You'll be famous. He'll make you an artist yet, youngster."

The painter's eyes were hot as he gazed after Borgia.

"I am an artist," he said, his voice small and tight.

Coffin's arms were seized by two serving men and he was led off in Borgia's wake, but as he went, he looked back over his shoulder at the boy's set face, and thought hard about what he saw there.

With a deep sigh of satisfaction, Nicholas lowered himself into the tub, splashing water out onto the stone flagged floor. At once the warmth of the water began to lessen the ache in his shoulder and ease the bone-biting chill that had settled on him during his trudge from Borgia's gate to Lalage's, the best whorehouse in Trastevere.

"Did you say something, signore?" a girl's voice asked.

He turned to look at the girl Lalage had sent down with him to the wooden tubs in the cellar. She was skinny and sallow, with a shock of black hair that hung untidily into her eyes. She brushed the tangle back with a grimy wrist and reached reluctantly for a lump of yellow soap and a sponge.

"Shall I start on your back, signore?" she asked, unenthusiastically.

"Please do. What's your name, girl?" Coffin asked.

"Serafina," she answered, wringing her sponge out over his shoulders. She ran the soap clumsily down his spine. Coffin judged she had little experience in washing, either others or herself, and little liking for the task.

"You can't have been here at Lalage's long," he said. And she wouldn't stay much longer, he added to himself. Lalage's girls were generally cleaner and always better looking. "Aren't you a bit young for this?"

"I'm thirteen," she said primly. "That's old enough."

"Why did Lalage send you? She knows my tastes. Not that you're not pretty," he lied, "but I generally have more in common with Lalage's more—mature—women."

"I know. But everyone else is tired. It's morning. Lalage says you ask for miracles—baths and laundry and fetching your friend. She said that from the looks of you when you came, I'd be safe enough. She says you like baths."

This last quotation was delivered in a tone of great skepticism.

"Thanks to the hot water and your attentions I feel much better, thank you, Serafina. You needn't rub the soap quite so hard, by the way. I'm sure you must be tired."

"I go to bed early. It's the other girls who have been up all night."

"That's enough scrubbing on my back, Serafina. Just rinse off the soap and I'll do the rest myself."

"Are you sure? Lalage said I was to help you."

"Very kind of Lalage. Would you do me the favor of going to see if my friend has come yet?"

"You're sure you don't want anything else?"

"Not now, Serafina. It's been a long night for me, too. Another time, perhaps."

"Well, all right. Lalage said Englishmen were different," Serafina remarked. She dropped the soap into the water with a splash and made for the door.

"I'm not that different, my girl," Coffin muttered, "but if I have an inch of skin left on my back it's not your fault."

He groped about the bottom of the tub for the soap, seized the sponge where it floated on the surface of the bathwater, and set about scrubbing his feet. When the door opened again, he spoke without looking up.

"Back so soon, Serafina? Then bring me something to drink and see if my clothes are dry."

"Do you know what time it is?" Angelo demanded. "It's morning. The sun is up. The birds are singing. I should be in bed asleep."

Nicholas looked up into the little man's pointed face.

"I've had a busy night too," he said soothingly. "Cesare Borgia sent for me."

"Santa Maria! No wonder you've got bruises."

"Indeed." Coffin nodded, and rinsed the film of soap suds away from the flamboyantly discolored bruises on his shoulder. "It was a long interview. When he let me go it was daybreak. He sent a man along to follow me in secret. Very considerate. To show my appreciation, I took the fellow down by the sewers. You know the spot, I'm sure, down by the river. It's really quite picturesque."

"Did he like it?" Angelo inquired.

"He must have. He never came back."

"Probably enjoyed himself so much he decided to stay. Still, with the crime in the streets these days, who knows?"

"Yes, isn't it terrible?" Nicholas sponged himself. "That's why I came to see Lalage. She's taken care of me many times."

"I can just imagine, Maestro—"

Angelo broke off as the door swung open and Serafina entered, a bundle of clothing under her arm.

"Lalage says here are your clothes. She says you can mend your own shirt."

"Thank you, Serafina. Could you see about something to drink for my friend and me?"

"I'll see what Lalage says." Serafina put the clothes down on a stool near the tub and flounced out.

When the door had closed, Angelo rolled his eyes.

"You want to be careful, Maestro. You'll be robbing cradles next."

"I'm going to be a little too busy for that in the next few days," Coffin said, face suddenly grim. "They've found Ercole's body. The funeral will be tomorrow night. I have until then to find the person who poisoned him."

"Tomorrow night! What if you can't find the killer by then?"

"Don't be naive, Angelo. He'll blame it on me. The Borgia family can't let something like this pass unavenged."

"But you didn't do anything. Well, you didn't kill him."

"I did enough," Coffin said, darkly.

Angelo swallowed, suddenly subdued.

"Two days isn't very long, is it?" he asked. "Except for the people who have to attend the corpse, I mean."

"No, it isn't. So if that girl ever gets back here we'll do our drinking and then go out for a good look at Giulietta's. The two of us should be able to cover it thoroughly. I want to know who goes in and who goes out—and when."

"You think she did it?"

"I hope so. The simpler this is, the better I'll like it."

CHAPTER NINE

The streets were emptied by noon drowsing and the lowering sky. Water filled the ruts made by the morning's traffic. Nicholas and Angelo picked their way across Trastevere back streets to the Palatine bridge, where the mud was ankle deep and Angelo floundered until he was splashed to the knees. Once across the Tevere, Coffin took the street of Santa Sabina and came up the Palatine hill as far as a narrow side street lined with elegant villas, each backed with its own walled garden. Steering Angelo into a doorway opposite, the Englishman hissed his directions into the cutpurse's ear.

"I want to know who comes and goes here. Look sharp and we'll both come out of this with whole skins."

"Sure we will, Maestro. Where will you be?"

"I want to know who comes and goes out the back, too. There's an alley running behind the gardens. I'll find a vantage from there."

"All I want to know is, who's going to come calling here at this hour of the day?" Angelo asked
plaintively.

"Isn't Giulietta one of Rome's loveliest women?
Or, at least, one of the most popular?"

"One of the fussiest, too. The light is too good to
hide a blush if she refuses to see you."

"Then keep your eyes open for whoever works
here. Get them talking if you can."

"That kind of talk comes easiest over a glass or
two."

"Whatever you have to do. Just *don't* try to be
clever. Only listen."

"Whatever you say, Maestro."

Nicholas watched the servants' entrance patiently for some time, counting the delivery boys as they
came and went. Evidently some evening entertainment was planned. Coffin watched the arrival of a
basket of fish, followed by the bread. The baker's
boy was punished for his tardiness by the cook,
who accepted the loaves, then sent him packing
with several well directed blows of a wooden
spoon. Under cover of this disturbance, Coffin
drew near the iron-grilled garden gate, estimating
its height. When the side door slammed, Nicholas
was up and over the gate with the speed of a cat.
Not risking the arrival of another delivery, he
crossed the garden at a dead run and clambered
among the ivy and olive trees until he had a grip on
the balustrade of the back balcony.

Congratulating Giulietta silently on the useful

frivolity of balconies, he turned his attention to the latch of the balcony door. He opened it with a dexterity that would have surprised and gratified Angelo.

The room he entered was spacious, furnished chiefly with a bed of magnificent proportions and an enameled bathtub shaped like a seashell. To his dismay, the tub was occupied by a dark-haired woman who eyed him with cool self-possession.

Coffin dropped his hand to the pommel of his dagger, saying softly, "Don't scream."

"I wasn't going to," the woman replied, raising a beautifully plucked eyebrow.

Coffin raised an eyebrow back at her.

"You are Giulietta, the mistress of this house, I presume," he asked.

"In this chamber? In this bath? Who but Giulietta?" she answered. She tilted her head back and squeezed her perfumed sponge so that the scented bathwater ran down her throat and over her breasts. Nicholas watched the water's progress appreciatively.

"My apologies, madonna," he said, "but I cannot permit you to leave your bath. If you should do so and manage to summon your servants, it would be most inconvenient for me."

"I had no intention of leaving my bath," Giulietta informed him coolly. "Why should I? And why should your convenience be of the slightest interest to me? I did not invite you here."

"I am here by request of Cesare Borgia."

"On the matter of his brother's death? How childish. I suppose he's ordered that I'm to be slain in my bath. Frankly, I would prefer the bite of an asp." Giulietta examined her fingernails critically as she spoke.

"Did you commit a crime worthy of execution?" Coffin countered. He crossed to the bedroom door and locked it.

"No," Giulietta replied, "which is more than darling Cesare can say, I'm sure."

"But you are not surprised to be questioned in regard to Ercole Borgia's death?"

"Poor little Ercole," she said, her voice low and gentle. "No. He was often with me."

"Did he dine with you the night before he was to have visited the Orsini family?"

"To deliver his deathless speech at that symposium? Yes. Heavens, how I coached him. He could not remember the last ten lines."

"Do you recall the menu?"

"Why, yes. My cook outdid herself. She liked Ercole and did her best for him, though he never noticed food. We had partridges and shellfish in wine."

"And what then?"

"What do you think?"

"I see. And then?"

"Then he left," Giulietta snapped.

"What time was this?"

"Morning," she said, her voice sharp. "Men do not generally leave me until I bid them to go." She found a hand mirror on the table beside the tub and studied her reflection grimly.

"Really? He was not seen."

"That does not mean a thing," she said disinterestedly.

"Where do you suppose he went, that he was not seen again alive?"

"How should I know?" she snapped. "Please unlock that door. I have a schedule to keep to. If my maid cannot fetch up more hot water, my bath will be delayed."

"Unthinkable," Nicholas assured her. He made no move to unlock the door. "Will you be able to spare the time from your schedule to attend the funeral? They found his body last night."

"Good, then you can go see the corpse and judge for yourself where he went, once they dry it out."

"Dry it out?" Coffin's voice was silky. "Why, madonna, they found his body in a shallow grave in one of the cemeteries outside the city wall."

Giulietta did not answer. She was busy retrieving the mirror she had dropped into the bathwater. When she had located it at the bottom of the tub, she brought it up and placed it on the table beside her. "My error," she said.

"I agree, madonna," Nicholas nodded. "I agree entirely." He sat down on the edge of her richly hung bed. "What did you talk about, madonna," he asked, "when the two of you were alone together? If, of course, it is not too painful a recollection."

Giulietta looked at him curiously, glanced to her table with its tray of soaps and sponges, looked back again at Coffin. "Trifles," she said at last. "The merest trifles. Mutual friends. Gossip."

"Did you quarrel?"

"No, not that I recall. We had little to quarrel about."

"He was, you will forgive me for observing, younger than you, madonna, was he not?"

"By several years. It did not greatly matter. Like most men, all he wanted was my complete attention. He was wealthy enough to command it. But he was also a pleasant person. Amiable."

"An unlikely personality trait in the Borgia family," Coffin said.

"You cannot know them well if you believe that," Giulietta replied. "Cesare can be disagreeable. Extremely disagreeable. But only when he feels his position is usurped. His position, you understand, is first in any company. As long as you treat him with complete respect he is deliberately agreeable, as if to make you look the fool for fearing him. Only, should the respect lapse, he becomes —impatient. Ercole was younger and less used to absolute obedience. Since he was accustomed to being outshone by Cesare, he could be quite pleasant."

"You know the family well."

"Cesare and I have met many times," Giulietta said, her voice distant.

"So, you have had some dalliance with him?" Nicholas ventured.

The question brought Giulietta's gaze sharply back to his face.

"Shepherds and shepherdesses dally. But I know what you mean. Precious few courtesans in Rome can say they haven't."

"He is a powerful man—I would say, unforgettable. Did you find him so? Perhaps you did. And perhaps Ercole became—what was the word you used earlier? Ah, yes. Inconvenient."

Giulietta's eyes flashed fire and for a moment Nicholas was certain she was going to throw the soap at him. Suddenly her gaze narrowed and she hissed, "Borgia never sent you here. I'd be dead by now if he thought I harmed his brother. You're a liar, foreigner, a bluffer and a liar."

Nicholas rose from the bed and put out a hand to stop her, but she slid through his grasp as she sprang from the tub. Distracted by her nudity, he misjudged her feint and she dodged to the door, unlatched it and threw it wide.

Before her first cry for help, he had made the balcony door and had it open even as the first servant cannoned into the bedroom. The seashell bath caught him across the kneecaps and sent him sprawling. Musk-scented bathwater sprayed ceilingward and cascaded onto the carpets. A second servant tripped over the first and skidded nose first across the damp rugs. Nicholas threw one last appreciative glance at Giulietta's damp curves and vaulted neatly over the balcony rail.

CHAPTER TEN

"There you are, Maestro," Angelo exclaimed. "I was looking for you. I've been here long enough. It's time I was home in bed. Long past time. As it is, I'll be a wreck tonight at work."

"Good thought, Angelo," Coffin replied. He picked himself up from where his leap from the garden wall had left him and took the little man's arm to propel him along as he made his way down the alley. "There's not much point in staying here."

Automatically, Angelo turned to look back for signs of pursuit.

"I had a little talk with the lady of the house," Coffin went on. "She may send a serving man or two to insure that we leave the neighborhood."

"Oh," Angelo nodded suddenly. "I see. I hope you got something good. I know a man who pays good money for—"

"Amazing as it may seem, I didn't steal anything. I just talked to her."

"Oh." Angelo's face fell. "Did she confess?"

Coffin frowned. "This isn't going to be that simple."

"I don't know if it will help, but I met a man—" Angelo began uncertainly, straining to keep pace with the tall Englishman.

"Who will pay good money for what?"

"Not that kind of man." Angelo looked reproachfully at Coffin. "He's one of Giulietta's servants. He knows all about who she has in and out of the house."

"Recently?"

"Very. He drinks at that wineshop near her house. He'll be there tonight."

"Are you sure?"

"Positive. I told him I knew a man who would pay very well for information."

"I should have known."

"So, that's that and we don't have anything left to do but sleep until it's time to meet him. So I'm going home to bed."

"Better not, Angelo."

"Maestro, I told you. I'll be a wreck if I don't get some sleep. You can't afford to pay me what it would cost to keep me awake any longer."

"If you go home now, you won't be alone. There are four men behind us, and I have a feeling they're going our way."

"Giulietta's henchmen?"

"No," Coffin replied. "Borgia's."

"Oh," Angelo said, and twisted back to peer over his shoulder.

"My friend doesn't seem to have enjoyed seeing

the city very much. Not even the sewers," Nicholas judged. "Ingrate."

Without breaking stride, Coffin sidestepped into an alley, pulling Angelo after him. He gauged the height of the wall beside them, and the pitch of the roof above that. Angelo followed his gaze consideringly and nodded his approval.

The hills of Rome make the roofs of the city a staircase, and Coffin scaled it, Angelo in tow.

Behind them, puffing slightly, came Borgia's men.

Their progress made its way from rooftop to balcony and up to gable. Where two houses stood too far apart for the cutpurse and the alchemist to leap, they bridged the gap with whatever came to hand: ladders, poles and piping. Over the crest of the Palatine, where the roofs thinned out to allow gardens their stately way, Coffin called a halt until the pursuit drew up with them.

Then, with the artistry of a hen partridge feigning injury to draw danger after her, Nicholas set out on the long sprint east through the open streets to the rotting hulk of the Colosseum.

Borgia's four men came on in hot pursuit.

"Keeping up nicely, aren't they?" Nicholas observed as he ran.

"They're breathing hard," Angelo pointed out.

"I don't suppose they get out much as a general rule. They should be grateful for the exercise," said Coffin.

Shoulder to shoulder, the pair vaulted up the slope to the nearest tumbled arches of the antique structure. There, within the shadow of the archway, they paused to watch the four men racing nearer.

"They should be," Angelo said, "but I'll bet they aren't."

The first of Borgia's men into the archway was the first man out, reeling backward from a well-placed right to the jaw. Nicholas nursed his knuckles and looked for the second man, who had stumbled over thin air—or Angelo's outstretched foot. The third man and the fourth stormed the arch a moment later and found it empty. They cast about in the myriad arched passages, but their quarry had vanished.

Only a few hundred feet away, but widening the margin fast, Nicholas and Angelo left the shadow of the great edifice and doubled back on their tracks. As they ran, Coffin shook his head.

"I've heard some very tough people live in there," he remarked with a jerk of his head back toward the Colosseum.

"Beggars," nodded Angelo. "Thieves and roughnecks."

"I do hope our friends don't meet any of them."

"Yes, because dressed as well as they are, the beggars and thieves would be sure to assume they were tax-collectors. That would be very uncomfortable for our friends, Maestro."

"They are probably tired of sightseeing by now, and will be glad of a change," Coffin said. "We can go home to sleep with a clear conscience, knowing we have fulfilled our duty."

"I could have gone home to sleep without that."

"Unfortunately, there is more at stake here than your capacity to sleep," Coffin retorted. "Where shall I meet you for our little interview tonight?"

"In the street of Santa Sabina, at the Sign of the Wolf. Our friend will meet us there just after the night watch goes out."

The cutpurse made a gesture of farewell, then looked back over his shoulder in the general direction of the Colosseum. With eloquent grace, he raised his right thumb to his nose and waggled four fingers. Then, as a horse-drawn cart loaded with beets rolled past, he vaulted up to a perch on the back of the cart and allowed it to bear him majestically away.

But Coffin did not turn for home, but rather sharp west to the nearest bridge on the Tevere. Once there, he doubled back on his tracks and struck off north, toward the Capitoline hill. Following a careful maze of back alleys and detours, he journeyed antwise through the strewn bones of the past until he reached the small piazza centered with the column of Trajan. He stopped briefly beside the monument, gazing up at the grim little figures spiraling their way up the column, then shifted his attention across the square to where, set among the stained facades of stone, was a wall with a great iron barred gate. Between the bars, Flamel's narrow garden could be glimpsed, overgrown with black cypress. Beyond the garden peeped a villa, nearly lost among the stiff unruly foliage.

He crossed the square and strode up purposefully to the gate. At his touch, the gate swung wide. He had never known it to be locked.

He passed through the garden with its little fountain in the shape of a lion's mask set into one wall.

The flow of water from its jaws had dwindled with time to an occasional drop sliding off its fangs, as though it still remembered the good old days in the Colosseum and let its mouth water senilely at the memory of Christians.

The garden gave way to a short flight of marble steps, treacherously worn, leading to the great door. As he expected, the latch was open. He entered silently.

After the garden, the villa's interior was impenetrably gloomy. Coffin paused a moment to let his eyes adjust, then picked his way carefully to the marble stair, more by memory than by sight.

As he climbed the stair his eyes began to give more information, but still they could not penetrate the dimness completely, and he succeeded only in perceiving the bulking outlines of the clutter he found here and there on the stairs and landings, unpleasantly crouching shapes that rustled or crackled ominously when he brushed against them. Steadfastly ignoring the unpalatable disorder, he continued, sometimes overstepping, sometimes sidling past the heaps of clutter, until he reached the top of the stair. There, a shaft of light lanced through the gloom, coming from beneath a narrow door. Nicholas knocked gently.

"Yes?" a voice called. "Come in, Nicholas, come in. Don't just stand there lurking."

He pushed the door open.

The room was spacious and well-lit, looking out directly into the garden and the piazza beyond. The light was somewhat dimmed, however, for the room was nearly filled with smoke, hanging pale blue and spice-scented in the air. At a table beside the window sat an old man, a supremely old man, the skin on his hands like ruched white silk as he held the mouthpiece of the water pipe that stood on the floor beside his chair. The old man nodded toward a chair across the room and took another puff on his pipe, his black eyes remote and glowing in their age-sunken sockets.

Nicholas took the chair offered him and stretched his legs out before him with a weary sigh.

"Good day, Flamel," he said. "Were you expecting me?"

"Not until I watched you trespass in my garden," the old man replied, his Italian slightly accented with French. He gestured to his pipe. "Would you care to join me?"

Nicholas declined courteously, having experience with the curious side effects the blue smoke elicited.

"I am involved in some rather urgent business," he said, "and would appreciate your counsel."

Flamel puffed meditatively as he regarded Coffin, black eyes taking him in from muddy boots to tousled hair.

"You smell of death," he said at last. "Have you killed someone, Nicholas?"

"No."

"I see." The black eyes looked beyond him into the past and the silence in the room grew as thick as the smoke.

Nicholas regarded the fragile little man crouched in the ornately carved chair and contrasted this with their first meeting.

It had been a year before, and he freshly come to Rome from honest England. He had traveled abroad before, lived the hard, brawling student's life from Paris to Bologna, cheating and being cheated from inn yard to lecture hall. Libraries lured him, and he had made his way from one to the other, pursuing the scattered fragments of an alchemical chimera. At last, he had come to Rome, following the rumor of a Frenchman named Flamel, who had once made gold from lead and had traveled on the proceeds to the far reaches of the Orient. From Alexandria to Shirilestan, Flamel had journeyed, purchasing what fragments he could of the great lost libraries of the east. Constantinople's fall to the Turk had brought him back, with half a Venetian galley's hold of caskets, trunks, and coffers filled with charred scrolls, age-scarred codices, and the components of exotic eastern vices. Though it was rumored that he had the philosopher's stone in truth, he lived in wonderful obscurity, for he was fabulously decrepit; and if he had wealth beyond his books and villa, it did not show. But the books alone were enough to draw Coffin, and he had visited the old man at his villa to ask him for permission to use his library. He had found Flamel in the garden, cleaning the moss off the fountain lion's mane.

"Library?" Flamel had wheezed. "You want to see my library?"

"Yes. I've journeyed across Europe to study with you."

"Wasted effort," Flamel said, with an emphatic scrape at the moss. "Why don't you try a university?"

"I have," Coffin answered gently.

"Oxford, I suppose, being English."

"Of course."

"The Sorbonne?"

"Naturally."

Flamel looked up at Coffin sharply and appeared to study him more closely.

"Bologna?" he asked. "And have you studied the library at Urbino? Very fine collection there."

"Yes," replied Coffin steadily.

"Liar," said Flamel. "The library at Urbino has almost nothing regarding alchemy. Now, the Academy at Florence, there you'd find something worth bothering with. Have you been to Florence?"

"It is my loss that I have not."

"You're right. It is." Flamel scraped moss industriously. "Why don't you go there and leave me alone? Florence is a lovely city, much preferable to Rome. Better climate, too."

"I intend to stay in Rome. I've traveled all the way from England to speak to you."

"Good God, why? You seem to be perfectly sound in mind and body. Why don't you find some honest work and leave mysterious hocus-pocus to old men who haven't anything more entertaining to do?"

"I don't seem to have an aptitude for honest work," Nicholas replied candidly. "I'm best at taking things apart, actually."

"You could aspire to become a butcher," the old man suggested reasonably.

"My temperament is not sufficiently phlegmatic to allow it. I don't care for killing things, though as a boy I was quite expert at dissecting bats and rabbits and finding out what caused their demise. But oddly enough, neither bats nor rabbits make a rule of dying of anything interesting enough to warrant all the work involved in taking them apart. So I went on to larger game. My father thought there might be some use to sending me away to school when I did. Even if there was no use, it made it easier to keep housemaids. They could hardly leave the house screaming in hysterics if I were sent to Oxford to dissect sheep, instead of doing it in the pantry."

"Your father sounds to me a remarkably tolerant man," Flamel responded, in a tone of great boredom.

"He was, and thought I might turn out to be a doctor, but at the university they made the fatal mistake of letting me into the library. After that, I had little patience with dosing the sick when the moon is in Aries and Mars is transiting Mercury. If willow bark cures a headache on Monday, it will cure it again on Tuesday. What I wanted to know was, what is it in willow bark that causes the cure?

That, of course, is not the kind of question encouraged by university lecturers. So I have searched for the answer where I could, and the answers to other questions as well. Some of the answers are found in alchemy, some in the writings of antique scholars. That is why I have been pursuing the search in libraries across Europe. My father's illness called me back to England, but just before he died rumors of your library reached England and the ears of the curate in our village. When he spoke to me of your journey in the Orient and the books you had found, I knew I had to come to Rome."

Flamel had scraped on methodically throughout this speech, but when Nicholas came to an end, the old man paused and glanced up, fixing him with a bird-like eye.

"You want the books badly enough to lie to me about Urbino, so God knows what else you've lied about. Still, such lies hurt no one, and with a little practice, you may become more expert. I enjoy a truly accomplished liar. Come when you wish and read my books. If you damage one, I will have your liver, needless to say. You would do well to leave me alone, and to deny that you have any dealings with me; otherwise you will find it difficult to find a place to live. I have a reputation bordering on the sinister. You would not benefit from association with me. As for answering your questions, rely only on the books. There's no use in hounding me. I'm an old man and possibly senile. Pay no attention to me."

Throughout the year, Nicholas had visited the

house in Trajan's piazza, picking his way through dozens of crumbling scrolls and codices. He had spoken often to Flamel, usually on days when the old man was either particularly affected by the contents of the water pipe or particularly scathing in regard to Coffin's intellectual pretensions.

But now, the old man seemed neither especially sedated nor unpleasantly sarcastic. He sat and puffed and gazed vaguely into the distance, and Nicholas felt emboldened to speak.

"Master Flamel," he began, "I am troubled by a matter of a poisoning. I've followed some of the methods I found recommended in your library: distillation, sublimation, calcination—"

"Been reading that ass Philalthis, eh?" Flamel demanded.

"Yes." Coffin confessed. "And I don't recognize the substance I've obtained."

"I suppose it's too much to expect you to confine your interests to alchemy, any more than you could resist distilling brandy into a clay aludel. That was your last problem, if I recall correctly."

Coffin stirred uncomfortably. Flamel went on.

"Couldn't you have analyzed this, er, substance, as you put it so delicately, before you tested it on some poor creature? Think of the time you would have saved."

"I hope I do not have to tell you that I did not administer the poison. I have, however, been given the responsibility of learning who did. It is my theory that I might better be able to tell who did the poisoning if I knew what the substance is and how it came to be administered."

"I don't like the tone of voice with which you tell me you have been 'given responsibility.' Are you in some sort of difficulty?" Flamel asked.

"If I were and had the audacity to admit it, you would speedily see me out of this house and probably bar the doors against me," Coffin pointed out.

"Quite correct. Not that I have any strong convictions against crime, mind." Flamel puffed reflectively. "It is simply not wise to consort with criminals at my age. Bad for one's financial security. If the forces of the law are pursuing you, Nicholas, you may show yourself out. I have no desire to sit here talking while Nemesis gains on you."

"I have committed no crime."

"Very well," Flamel sighed. "I suppose you will refuse to leave until you have had your little problem discussed to your satisfaction. Perhaps if it is speedily solved you will be on your way before the forces of retribution find you here and disturb my domestic tranquillity." Flamel puffed industriously for several minutes. "Tell me about this substance, Nicholas."

"The body was blue," Coffin began.

"How nice," Flamel's gaze took on an absent quality.

"Quite an intriguing shade of blue," Nicholas offered coaxingly.

"I have seen such things before now," Flamel replied in a lofty tone.

"I dared to hope as much."

"Don't be misled by the obvious symptom," Flamel advised. "Nor, indeed, by any symptom. Concentrate on the substance itself. You tell me you have allowed it to sublimate?"

"I had hoped to allow it to sublimate in the neck of the alembic," Nicholas nodded. "Unfortunately, try though I will, I cannot get it to do so."

"Trying too hard will force an erroneous result. If it does not sublimate, it is not arsenic."

"We make progress. It is not arsenic." Nicholas ticked off a finger. "It is not antimony. I checked for that. What else isn't it?" He ticked off a second finger and looked up expectantly.

"I doubt that the process of elimination is a suitable approach to the problem," Flamel said. "I greatly fear that unless an additional amount of the substance is obtained we will be unable to identify it."

"It leaves a green residue. I burned a small amount and produced a green tint in the flame," Nicholas offered. "That should eliminate quite a few possible choices."

Flamel paused with his mouthpiece halfway to his lips.

"Green?" he asked. Coffin nodded. The old man tilted his head to one side and took a meditative puff. After a dreamy contemplation lasting several minutes, he blew a smoke ring and spoke.

"You must not take the word of an old man, for my memory is very likely faulty. I have so much more to remember than most. But should you by some chance find a specimen of the substance in the course of your, er, research, it may well appear in the form of an alkaline earth, sometimes found refined into a silver-colored metal. There are books here that could confirm your findings, should it be so. Bear in mind that this is only a guess, made by a man of advanced years. The merest speculation."

"You recognize the poison?" Nicholas exclaimed. "You know what it is?"

"Calm yourself, Nicholas. Cultivate patience."

"Flamel! My ability to cultivate anything is going to be severely impaired unless I find that poison very soon. You know what it is—"

"I know what I think it is, but it will do you no good to leap to conclusions. If I give you a name, you'll influence your findings to agree. No, objectivity is essential. You must not only solve your problem, but learn from the solution."

"My objectivity is already strained," Nicholas pointed out plaintively. "My life is in danger unless I identify the poison and the poisoner."

"Dear me, Nicholas," said Flamel, with a look of reproach. "You assured me you were not in any difficulty with the law. How upsetting."

"Tell me what you know," Coffin demanded, "or I will see to it that your household receives a visit from several curious cutthroats in the employ of Cesare Borgia."

"That upstart," sniffed the old man. "Be reasonable, my boy. If I tell you what I know, why, it could take years."

"You know perfectly well—" Nicholas began, exasperated.

"Decades," Flamel corrected himself.

Coffin forced himself to relax and lean back into his chair. Lips set in a straight line, he eyed Flamel grimly.

"You have other lines of inquiry to pursue in

this matter, do you not?" the old man asked. "What will it gain you to intimidate me?"

"The poison," he replied curtly.

"But I have said I am only guessing. You saw the substance, not I. A mere name will not enable you to identify the killer."

"No, but I can try to find out where the killer obtained the poison, and question the supplier. If it were arsenic, for example—"

Flamel sighed.

"Oh, my dear boy. What a stupid idea."

"Is it? My time is limited, true, but I have contacts—"

"Do you? Contacts enough to allow you to question every apothecary in the city? And if you did, what makes you think this particular poison is doled out by druggists?"

Coffin opened his mouth and closed it again. The old man had not taken a puff from his pipe in several minutes. Uninterrupted, he might continue to speak to the point.

"I take it that your silence is an admission that you have no reason to think so," Flamel went on. "You astonish me. If you are so impatient to discover who the poisoner is, why do you not deduce his identity? I should think it would be child's play compared with questioning every source of supply in the city. Or any source, rather. I'll be surprised if you can find one."

Nicholas lifted his eyebrows and waited, holding his breath in anticipation.

"If the poison were barium salts, now, what would you think of that? Whom would you question? How many sources of supply are there?" demanded Flamel.

"Barium?" Nicholas repeated blankly. "What in the world is barium?"

"Barium salts. It's a poison, obviously. It has its uses, I suppose, but how you plan to track down a purchaser mystifies me, I admit."

"What uses does it have?" inquired Nicholas faintly. "Is it something a man might have come into contact with accidentally?"

"I doubt it. When I visited the Orient, I was told of it for the first time. The natives of Cathay celebrate their New Year with displays of gunpowder and explosives fired into the air. Different substances are used to cause the smoke and fire resulting to assume various colors. Most impressive. Barium is responsible for the green hue."

"An unlikely source for Roman poison."

"It must have other uses," Flamel said. "Somewhere in my library, you're certain to come across a mention of it."

"Unfortunately, I have a limited command of Oriental languages," snapped Nicholas.

"Impatience is hardly the spirit in which to approach this matter," Flamel reminded him. "Suppress it, and you will notice an immediate improvement in fortune. Observe the salutary effect holding your tongue had on me. I did not intend to inform you of my guess, but as you insisted on pursuing the wrongest possible line of thought, I could hardly keep silent. Oh, I scarcely need mention that such a method will not work a second time with me, do I? Good. Then I really think,

Nicholas, that if you do not have time to waste on my books—and I use the word 'waste' with great distaste—you do not have time to sit here and clutter up my room. So I advise you to be on your way, for you will get no more of me today."

So saying, Flamel applied himself earnestly to his pipe, black eyes narrowed into slits.

"I know you too well to suppose you will relent and offer to help me," Nicholas said with resignation. "I admit, though, I am interested in learning how you intend to be rid of me."

As he spoke, the old man's head sagged forward until his chin nearly touched his chest. One claw-like hand joined the other in his lap, and the mouthpiece of the pipe fell unnoticed beside the chair.

"I see," said Coffin. "You have fallen asleep, victim of your advanced years, and will catnap senilely until I've gone. I imagine in time your pipe will go out and that will goad you into dropping this charade. Meanwhile, I am to take myself off and deduce who committed the crime. 'Child's play,' I believe you said. Very well. Good day. Don't bother to rise. I'll see myself out."

Beyond the gentle rise and fall of the old man's chest, Coffin received no reply.

CHAPTER ELEVEN

Sleeplessness was starting to affect him, manifesting itself in muscle aches and a buzz within his skull. With the promise of mattress and blanket to spur him, he made it up the flight of stairs to his rooms and unlocked the door by focusing his entire attention on the simple interplay of key in lock.

Once inside, the room was filled with light spilling blindingly in the far window. For a moment he didn't see the woman who sat at his table, a basket before her, but when she rose to meet him, the sun struck white fire off her hair.

"Costanza!" he exclaimed, his voice uneven. He cleared his throat, tried again. "What are you doing here?"

She stepped forward and put out her arms to steady him.

"I was afraid," she answered simply.

He found himself sitting on the edge of the bed, Costanza beside him. Her warmth took some of his chill fatigue away.

"My dear, where have you been?" she asked. "I came last night and you weren't here. I came this morning and you weren't here. I came an hour ago, still nothing. Your landlady told me you were gone."

"She did?" he asked blankly.

"She let me in and told me I could wait but that you had never come back last night. She heard you'd been arrested. I thought—"

"What?"

"Nothing." She looked down at her clasped hands. "I told the servants I was going to mass. Ludo has another dinner this evening, but I shouldn't stay—not much longer."

Nicholas raised her chin so that he could meet her eyes.

"There's no secret about the fact that I'm in trouble," he said, "but there's nothing you can do to help. Do you understand? Nothing. All I can accomplish by telling you where I've been is to put you in danger. You're in danger right now, being here, knowing me. You have no idea how difficult things may become."

"You're right. I don't." Costanza took his cold hands in her warm ones. "Hadn't you better tell me?"

"I can't."

"You won't. Bianca said you'd been arrested. You haven't denied that."

"I can't deny that."

"Why would they arrest you? Is it because you study with that horrible old Frenchman? You've done that for months."

"You'd do better to ask why, if I was arrested last night, I'm free today."

"I know better than to ask since you wouldn't tell me. But it's no surprise. You are Nicholas Coffin, an Englishman on chatting terms with the devil. The surprise would be if they could keep you where you didn't want to be."

"Costanza, this is not a game of gulling husbands and tricking pawnbrokers. This is serious and I don't have time to waste arguing with you."

"Or time to waste on food or sleep, from the looks of you."

Nicholas shook his head impatiently. Costanza cut in before he could speak.

"Look, don't trust me. Don't tell me. I don't care. Only don't try to tell me you don't need any help. There's food in that basket, and anything else you want—" her voice faltered, "—is here too."

Nicholas took her by the wrists and shook her.

"You little idiot—don't you hear me? Just coming here is foolish. Your 'help' can get you killed. *Do* you understand?"

She stopped struggling and went limp in his arms. Her head rested on his shoulder; her lashes drooped languorously.

"If I'm in danger here," she murmured, "I'd be in more danger leaving now. And since you say you don't have much time, it would be wise not to waste more of it quarreling, don't you think?"

"I thought you had to leave to save the lie you told."

"I'll tell them I had to make a long confession."

"Can't you get a serious thought inside your

head?" He shook her again, angrily. "You are in danger here."

Her arms curled around him, her breath warm on his neck.

"Then protect me, darling Niccolo."

"Stupid woman! This is no time for that."

"I thought there was always time for that."

His last shake had loosened her hair pins irrevocably and now her blonde hair came down in a torrent over her shoulders and down her back. His fingers tangled in the silk of it, and he found himself quite unwilling to pull away.

"Witch!" he said, despairingly. "Then you've brought it on yourself."

Costanza seemed untroubled by any of his words.

He was alone when he awoke, vaguely able to remember stirring when she had left his arms. Her clothes were gone, of course. He rubbed his hand across his eyes and sat up. Every trace of her was gone except her basket and a single hair pin lost in the tangle of bedclothes beside him. A look out the window reassured Coffin. The rich royal blue of twilight still lingered over the rooftops.

He pulled his shirt back on with a sigh, then raked his fingers hastily through his hair. The hamper looked too promising to wait until his points were tied, so he simply pulled on his thick hose and left their fastening for after his investigation of the basket.

Costanza seemed to have done more than simply order a basket of bread and cheese. Only her personal attention for a period of several hours could have produced such a selection of delicacies. Her concern for him had evidently taken the form of an extended bout in the kitchen. The basket contained bread, certainly, and some rather smelly goat cheese, but there was also half a roast chicken, a small earthenware crock of liver paste, a larger crock of figs in honey, and a cheese tart rich with eggs and cream.

After demolishing half the tart and a chicken leg, his hunger had subsided to a degree that allowed him to finish dressing. He tied his points, adjusted his trunks and codpiece, then pulled on his soft leather boots. He tucked in his torn shirt, then hesitated.

No knowing, of course, what sort of work the night might bring. But if he was to be one of Angelo's high-paying gentlemen, he might as well look the part. With a smile of satisfaction, Coffin kicked his old jerkin into the corner and from the chest at the foot of his bed withdrew his best doublet and cap. Both were dark blue, the cap of velvet and the doublet of wool. The doublet's shoulders were slightly old fashioned, being wide and deeply padded, but the padding added warmth and the collar of the doublet was marten fur, warm and fashionable. He laced himself into the thick soft wool and adjusted the soft blue cap at a rakish angle. The sleep had restored him greatly, and the clean clothing raised his morale. He felt more eager for questions and questionings than he had in the past day and night. He was thirsty enough to consider drinking the clean water left in the crockery pitcher but decided not to chance it and simply poured the water into the basin to splash his face and hands clean. Thirst, he promised himself, could be better handled where he and Angelo had agreed to meet.

On the walk to the wineshop Nicholas took the street of Santa Sabina nearly all the way, but was forced to detour into a parallel street when he found his way blocked. The offending party was a troop of Indian Musselmen and the elephant they attended. Haughty courtiers hovered about giving advice but the elephant paid no heed. Despite all the urging of the trainers, the beast refused to continue on, sidling with ponderous daintiness from one side of the street to the other.

"It'll be the coldness of the mud on her feet that's making her fash herself," said one of the Indian keepers in an incongruously Scots accent. "That, and the torches they're waving about since it's grown dark. She dislikes the smoke."

"She's a largish creature," Nicholas observed.

"That she is," replied the keeper with pride. "They sent for her all the way from the King of France's menagerie to be part of the Twelfth Night procession, and while she's here she's to march along in the funeral procession tomorrow midnight."

"Funeral?" Coffin repeated the word automatically but the elephant's gambolings brought her near and the keeper skipped out cricket-like to steer her on her way.

Until that moment, Coffin had put out of his

mind the proximity of Ercole's funeral. Now, as he watched the exotic beast that would be part of the great cortege, he realized that the following night loomed abominably close. As he looked across to where the elephant stamped and sidled in the mud, one of the smoking torches flared in a keeper's hand. There, lit for an instant by the snapping pitch, stood one of Borgia's men. Still clad in his bull-badged livery, though the fabric was now stained and torn, he was the man Coffin had last seen tripping over Angelo's foot at the Colosseum.

Step by step, Coffin glided back into the shadows, leaving the liveried man watching the elephant intently. Sure-footed despite the icy mud, Coffin melted into the darkness of a narrow side street and continued on his way to the Sign of the Wolf.

One again, in Giulietta's brocade curtained dining room, candles flared bright in their sconces. This time there were musicians, two slender boys with viols. As they played, the five men ranged about the table watched one another in wary silence while Giulietta chose a sample of the first course, and presented it on its silver dish to her chosen taster. Gingerly, the servant selected a morsel of white fish, glistening in pale wine sauce, and ate it. When he had swallowed he looked hopefully at Giulietta.

"All of it," she said, flatly.

He ate the rest slowly and then drank the glass of wine she poured out for him. In reply to her questioning look, he spoke.

"It's good, madonna."

"Excellent." She inclined her head graciously. "You may serve us."

Around the table he went, portioning out the flaky white fish onto the intricately painted plates and brimming the Venetian goblets with wine. For several moments, the attractions of the table took up all their attention, but presently one of the guests put down his ivory handled knife.

"An Epicurean repast," he said, raising his wine glass in a salute to his hostess.

"It is the first course only, Count Pitti," she reminded him, with a little nod to acknowledge his uplifted glass.

"But certainly there are more resemblances here to the splendor of antique Rome than the menu alone," the Count insisted. "Splendid surroundings, splendid company—"

"Splendid conversation," broke in a second guest sardonically. Ludovico Falchi was a noted scholar and philosopher, and an ornament to any social gathering, but a single glance about the table at his fellow guests had forced him to admit he was neither the wealthiest nor the youngest of the assembly. His disappointment at this observation served only to make him wish to be as caustic as etiquette would permit, at his fellow guests' expense, if possible.

"As you say, Signore Falchi," Giulietta nodded. "Indeed, we are in distinguished company." She gazed around the table. "In our number we find a poet, a scholar, a soldier, a nobleman, and a cardinal. Every walk of life is represented, is it not?"

"A veritable pantheon," Cardinal Galliano agreed. "Even as you have the gods and goddesses depicted on these plates. A clever conceit. I suppose I was allotted Pluto and Proserpina because my vocation concerns, in part at least, the life beyond this one?"

"And I was allotted Apollo in honor of my poetic profession," added Tonio Bianchi, the season's most fashionable new poet.

"Then I do think I might have had a more fitting subject than Neptune," objected Francesco di Rimini, Rome's latest and most dashing mercenary captain. He had no classical learning, but had seen a fountain ornamented with just such a figure that morning. Fortunately, he had asked about it, and now put his military talent for bluffing to good use.

"For such a notable soldier, sir, my Mars would be the wisest choice," Giulietta conceded. "But he is so neatly entangled with Venus I could not bear to part them. And I am entitled to Venus, am I not?"

"Indisputably," Falchi said. To Francesco he added, "You might console yourself that Neptune was as good a horseman as you are said to be. My assigned god, or hero, rather, would also suit a soldier, being Hercules, a notable warrior. Yet let me keep him, for he was a philosopher too in some ways. He had to choose between Virtue and Pleasure, as we all must."

"And which did he choose?" Francesco asked

with interest, but his question was lost as Count Pitti joined in, having racked his brains to identify the goddess adorning his plate and think of something appropriate to say.

"If you desire a scholarly divinity, Signore Falchi," he burst out at last, "you need not stretch a point to get Hercules into it tail first, for here's Minerva, goddess of wisdom, and I cannot for the life of me see what I have in common with her."

"Nor can I," Falchi replied.

Briskly, Giulietta clapped her hands to summon the next course, and in the ritual of tasting and serving and replenishing the wine, the thread of conversation was lost.

As Falchi disjointed a chicken wing a few moments later, he watched his hostess carefully move a delicate goblet aside a split second before Count Pitti's elbow would have swept it off the table. She then selected the correct utensil from her place setting and speared a morsel of chicken, to Francesco's obvious relief, as he had been staring at the elegant setting before him with dismay for several minutes, trying to deduce just which delicate implement would be proper to employ. Tonio was taking advantage of an abundance of wine his poet's income did not allow him to experience often, and in so doing, spilt a half glass of pale wine on the snowy damask of the table cover. The scholar shifted his attention to Cardinal Galliano, who was dismembering a chicken quarter with single-minded concentration, and devouring it in such haste that Falchi began to revise his chances for the

evening. With leisurely grace he blotted his lips on
the damask napkin in his lap and took up his wine
glass. No, it began to appear as though it might be
quite a profitable evening after all.

CHAPTER TWELVE

"There's the man." Angelo nudged Coffin out of the doorway and pointed to a large man who appeared to be drinking with great concentration. "Tubby, there. His name is Duccio."

Coffin made his way between the tables and benches and slid into a place close by the silent man, as he crouched over his bottle.

"Good evening, Duccio," he said. This drew no response but Coffin went on amiably. "Good, then I'll join you. Another round?"

"You're the man Angelo knows?" Duccio asked, looking up blearily from his drink. "You'd better pay well."

"I'm Angelo's friend," Coffin said.

Duccio eyed Coffin's doublet appraisingly.

"You'd better make this worth my while. I got sacked for talking to Angelo today," he said, and upended his wine cup.

"What happened?"

"Somebody got in the house while I was out for a glass or two. How was I to know somebody would try to get inside in broad day? He must have been crazy."

"That's bad luck for you."

"It sure is. Who'd have thought she'd be so choosy about who she wants to see? Keeps herself like a jewel in a box. Picky as a countess." Duccio went on mumbling disjointed sentences, leaning closer and closer to his drink, so that his speech was less and less intelligible.

Coffin prudently emptied the remainder of the bottle's contents into another cup and took charge of it himself.

"Choosy, is she?" he asked, attempting to keep the man awake. "Funny trade for a choosy woman."

Duccio lifted his bloodshot eyes to Coffin's face and began to laugh, an unpleasant wheezing sound.

"Choosy?" Duccio repeated, "I should say she's choosy. This last three months she's changed men like she changes her earrings, but every one is judged as carefully as blooded breeding stock. There was a cardinal, old but wealthy. When he dropped dead at mass one day, she went on to a country boy, a painter, just in from some northern town. Faenza, that was it. He made a little money, got a little work, then she got him. You know, I feel sorry for them sometimes. Most of them just think with their balls anyway, but you'd think for what she costs them, they'd be treated right so if they do go to hell, at least they go happy. But no, here comes this puppy fresh into the city, who takes one look at her and follows her home with a look on his face like a happy tomcat on the town. From the day they met, the only work he got done was on her portrait. All he did was try to please her, yet they fought like dog and bitch morning and night."

"They must have argued rather loudly. You seem quite up to date with his grievances. What did they quarrel about?"

"Oh, his work, her work. You know the kind of thing. When she felt neglected, she would talk about his earnings and make him feel small. Tell him what she could be getting if he weren't so unreasonable. He'd shout, threaten to kill anyone who touched her."

"Oh, really?"

"You know these farm boys. She got tired of him after awhile, found somebody richer, just as young."

"That would be the Borgia?"

"Yes." Duccio put his wine cup down and looked about abstractedly. "But that's done with now. She'll have to find someone else. There's a dinner tonight, in fact."

"Who are her guests?"

"Oh, everyone. Some rich men, some fashionable men, some old men. They'll all gas on about beauty. Pretty soon she'll get bored and pick one and the rest will get drunk and go home. If they get on, well, she'll have another man to pay for the partridges and parsnips."

"Is Cesare Borgia invited?"

"Borgia?" Duccio looked surprised. "If he wanted her, she'd know. He's not subtle. And he never goes to boring parties." Duccio's eyes narrowed. "You're pretty full of Borgia, aren't you?"

"Let's just say I have an interest in the subject. Tell me about Ercole Borgia. Did he fight with Giulietta?"

Duccio stirred uncomfortably. He looked around the room and rubbed the back of his neck as if to provoke thought.

"Look," he said finally, "I don't know who you are, but I have to go. You may be interested in the subject of Borgias, but I'm interested in staying alive. So just pay me now and I'll buy you a drink next time I see you."

Before Coffin could reply, the fat man was out of his seat and on his way to the door. Coffin was after him immediately but the press of people held him back. Before he reached the center of the room, Duccio was out the door.

Frowning savagely, the alchemist pushed through the crowd toward the door. With magical suddenness, Angelo materialized at his side.

"Don't look now, Maestro, but we've got friends here." Angelo nodded significantly toward the chimney corner.

Coffin did not have to follow Angelo's glance to the corner to know whose men were there.

"Duccio left without even waiting for his money, just as we were getting to some interesting points. It would be a shame if our friends followed us and took him away when we found him. They'd take him to see their master, and Duccio would probably end up seriously damaged before he convinced them he was only an innocent informer." Coffin continued to sidle toward the door as he spoke. "So, Angelo, our friends cannot come along with us this time. It's rude to disappoint them just when they've come to depend on us to show them a good time, but they've got to be kept here."

Angelo looked at Coffin dubiously.

"How long?" he asked.

"Long enough for me to catch up with our fat friend and take him somewhere quieter."

Angelo's eyebrows rose.

"While *you* catch him? You mean I have to do this alone?"

"I'm sure you'll be fine. At any rate, I refuse to ruin my last decent piece of clothing in a lowly tavern brawl. Therefore, Angelo, in payment for the wonderful gift you brought to my door and sold me—yes, you work alone."

Coffin's gaze held Angelo's for a moment, until the cutpurse gave an expressive shrug. He reached out stealthily with his left hand and plucked a purse as if it were a cherry, then transferred it to the cuff of a richly trimmed tunic.

"Thievery here!" he bellowed. "I saw it with my own eyes. Sir, your purse is gone, I saw the hand that took it—No, but the scoundrel can't have gone far. . . ."

Coffin reached the door just as the purse fell from its precarious hiding place to the floor. A howl went up and the press of merrymakers became a roaring mass of arms and legs. One of Borgia's men rose and started for the threshold, only to be engulfed in the human tide. The others were pinned in their corner by the mass of bodies. Crockery was thrown. Clothing was torn away and thrown into the air. Angelo made his way through the roiling bodies, harvesting a purse here and a jeweled pin there as bodies hurtled past.

Outside in the street, Coffin was well away.

Duccio squandered his lead looking for a likelier wineshop, and became aware he had been followed only when Coffin's hand fell heavily on his shoulder.

"Now," the Englishman purred, "where shall we go that's private? You're quite right about not speaking to strangers in crowded places. I think we should find somewhere more secluded."

He steered the fat man into an alley and backed him up until his shoulder blades scraped the wall.

"Let's talk about you, Duccio," he said gently.

"Me?" Duccio's voice was thin.

"You. What exactly were your duties in La Bella Giulietta's household?"

"I made sure no one came in who wasn't supposed to, and that no one stayed after they weren't welcome," Duccio answered.

"And?"

"And I served at dinner and tasted the food."

"You what?" Coffin's voice went suddenly small.

"I tasted the food. She has plenty of competition. Lots of ladies in her line of work would be glad to hear she got sick or had her skin go bad."

"When was the last night you tasted the food?"

"Last night."

"You did it every night?"

"It was my job."

"Do you remember the last night Ercole Borgia was there?"

"Yes," Duccio's voice was cautious.

"Tell me about it."

"There was partridges in a kind of sticky sauce, and mussels in wine, and roast mutton. I didn't like the mutton."

"And?"

"That's all."

"Don't be an idiot. Forget about food for a moment. Was there anyone there other than Giulietta and Borgia and yourself?"

"No. I wasn't even there the entire time. Just at the beginning of the meal. I brought in each course and tasted it from the main serving dish—"

"Right from the dish?" Coffin interrupted.

"No, the mistress has a little silver dish she scoops a portion into. I ate out of that."

"Then?"

"Then I served up their plates. As usual, I didn't taste anything odd in the food or fall down sick, and they let me go."

"Did you taste anything strange?"

"No. Not that night. Once I thought I'd been poisoned for sure but it was only some new idea of the mistress's—she had bought some kind of dried spice from the Indies—capsicum. She had cook put it in a sauce. I thought I would die for certain, but she said it was supposed to taste that way. It was expensive, too."

"What happened after you served them that night?"

Duccio's response was slow in coming.

"I went down to the kitchen," he said at last. "I was hoping to get the last of the mussels in wine, but all that was left was mutton."

"And?"

"Stop saying 'and?' all the time," Duccio snapped suddenly. "I can't think."

"Then don't," Coffin retorted. "Just talk."

"I cleared off the serving things after they were done and had gone upstairs."

"Is that all?"

"Yes."

"Did you see them again that night?"

"No."

"Did you see Borgia leave in the moring?"

"No. I never paid attention to things like that. It wasn't my job."

"Was Borgia planning to come back to see Giulietta?"

"You would, wouldn't you? Or maybe you've never seen her. Well, just take my word for it, if she sent you off on your way with a kiss some fine morning, you'd plan to come back as soon as you could. Depend on it."

"What do you think happened to Borgia?"

"I think somebody dragged him into an alley someplace and he never came out."

"Be glad someone took you into one," Coffin told him, handing him a silver piece. "Conversations like this are much more comfortable in the open air than in some stuffy dungeon. So look sharp when you go, and don't talk to strangers. Especially not four strangers who travel together and might follow you home. Stay in the alleys if you can."

Duccio bit his coin and nodded his thanks. Wordlessly, he turned and made his way into the darkness.

Coffin turned to reach the street again, but found his progress blocked by a pair of silent figures.

"I told you I heard money," one said to the other. "I can smell the stuff."

The speaker stepped forward, as Coffin did the same. The alchemist came in under his attacker's arm and shifted his weight, throwing the man smoothly over his shoulder into the alley mud. The second figure hung back for a moment, then spoke as Coffin turned to face him in a fighter's crouch.

"Ah, no, Maestro," Aldo said. "My apologies, but I will not fight with you. The moonlight is so dim, and my partner so careless, we mistook you. Again, my apologies."

Coffin turned back to glare at the thug he had already attended to. Aldo read his thought.

"No, not the same partner. I've been having bad luck keeping them lately, and you seem to have been a little hard on this new one. Too bad. He showed promise, too."

"In the future, Aldo," the Englishman chided him, "I'd suggest you work alone. Your partners seem to have a tendency to lose their balance."

"You are right, as always, Maestro. It is the mud, you know. Ice and mud are treacherous, for one in my line of work. Hard on the knees, too. Well, my friend," Aldo shifted his attention to his partner, who was now beginning to show signs of life, "meet Maestro Nicholas Coffin."

The evening, Francesco told himself, looked like a loss. There were plenty of beautiful women in Rome, and no reason to feel embarrassed if this particular woman was simply too expensive. He had an inkling of the fact when he had arrived, for the costly simplicity of Giulietta's gown, and the size of the ruby in the brooch nestled between her breasts, were something he had no experience with. Perhaps later on in his career, but for now he knew he could not afford the price of staying to see the evening to a close. It was unfortunate, but perhaps inevitable, for the company had been a bit above him from the start. The women he knew in Rimini did not give dinners for their suitors and expect them to chat politely the night through. Nor, he conceded, did they provide food and drink on a level comparable to what he had seen. Still, it was most unsettling to be expected to sit down and talk while eating. And not even to talk strategy, either. He had been fortunate to be able to recognize the character of Neptune. It would have proved most embarrassing to have listened to the conversation in total silence. He sipped his wine and consoled himself that, given the pretentious atmosphere, it was only to be expected that the lady had chosen the most pretentious of her guests to single out for her attention. Francesco eyed the scholar with disfavor. He wasn't much to look at, neither young nor old, with short cropped, mousy hair. He was also extremely pale and had grown mercifully silent in the past hour. Perhaps, Francesco thought hopefully, the dinner had disagreed with him.

Galliano looked up from his plate at last and popped his only remaining meat tart into his mouth. Smacking his lips softly, he drained his wineglass and looked expectantly about him.

The boys in the corner went on playing their viols monotonously and no other servants attended the table, either to pour wine or bring on yet another course. The cardinal eyed Falchi's plate with its nearly untouched tarts and sighed enviously. Giulietta paid no attention. She seemed unable to take her eyes off the scholar's face, although she still nodded absently in response to Count Pitti's pleasantries. Tonio drowsed charmingly over his wine cup, having long since given up the attempt to speak across Galliano's girth and engage his hostess in conversation.

The scholar passed a trembling hand across his forehead. Yes, Francesco decided, he certainly looked ill. He noted with some satisfaction that the man's breathing was shallow and irregular, then realized that Giulietta herself had paled and was ignoring the Count to bend solicitously over Falchi.

"My dear sir," she exclaimed, "are you ill?"

"It's nothing," the scholar murmured. "A slight headache, nothing more."

"Certainly not slight, sir." Giulietta responded crisply. She clapped her hands and a servant materialized in the doorway.

"Please assist Signore Falchi to a guest chamber.

He is ill and must not be allowed to risk himself in the street on the way home. The night is cold."

The servant nodded and joined her at Falchi's side. A second serving man entered and went to Tonio where he sat over his empty wine cup. Giulietta went on.

"I will see to Signore Falchi; you need not trouble yourself on his behalf, nor delay your departure further. I know how unpleasant it is in the evening streets, and how expensive it is to hire a chair to bear you home, so I understand your desire to leave."

Tonio was aided to rise and propelled toward the door on the servant's arm. With assorted protestations, Galliano, Pitti, and Francesco were escorted after him by servants who deftly provided them with the cloaks and gloves they had arrived in. At the doorway, Francesco paused and looked back at Giulietta's dark-eyed, expensive beauty, hovering above the ashen-faced scholar. Yes, he judged, he really must remember that gambit in the future. Perhaps his next campaign would prove lucrative enough to allow him to put it to use. An interesting pallor could be extremely rewarding, it was plain.

CHAPTER THIRTEEN

As he had done two nights before, Coffin stood in the doorway fragrant with urine and wet straw and pounded on Basilio's door.

This time Basilio himself answered the door, opening it a hand's breadth and peering cautiously out into the gloom.

"You, Englishman?" he exclaimed. "Come to borrow my shovel again?"

"I've come to borrow your memory," Nicholas replied curtly. "Let me in."

Basilio stood back and let Nicholas move past him into the low-ceilinged room. Once inside, Coffin turned and watched the graverobber bolt the door behind him.

"It's not much," Basilio gestured about him when he had finished with the door, "but it's yours if you need it, Coffin."

"Thank you, Basilio." Coffin's dark eyes met the graverobber's gaze and held it a moment. "Our ex-

pedition the other night put you into enough danger on my account. I've only come for some information this time. You haven't had any trouble
about the other night, have you?"

"None to speak of, though I have taken care not
to work that side of the city since."

"Good work."

"So. Information, Englishman?" Basilio mo-
tioned Coffin to a seat on the room's one bench.
He took a stool and seated himself within the circle
of light cast by his oil lamp.

"If you can give it to me," Coffin said. "Do you
remember telling me you sold cadavers to painters?"

"I remember."

"You know a lot of painters, then?"

"A lot? I know them all. There's not a painter
worth the hair in his brushes that doesn't come to
me. And what they don't tell me about themselves
isn't worth knowing. I don't know what comes
over them—something about corpses makes them
nervous or something. I don't know what it is exactly, but they surely do talk."

"Have you ever heard of a young painter who
came here from up north, not long ago? He's from
Faenza, they tell me, and he got taken up by
Giulietta, the courtesan."

"Are you talking about Lorenzo di Faenza? He
was with Giulietta."

"Lorenzo?" Coffin leaned forward on the bench
in his eagerness. "You know him?"

"Well, yes," Basilio replied, "but don't eat me."

"Sorry," Coffin said, leaning back.

"What do you want to know about him?"

"Everything."

"That's going to take awhile. He was very nervous."

"I've got time."

"Like you say, he came to Rome from Faenza not too long ago. His family is important there, he tells me—though whatever it's worth to be important in Faenza, I wouldn't know. So, they have their own private little guild up there—you know the kind, with Papa Nico and Uncle Pico and Grandfather Rico, and everybody's sister's husbands all working elbow to elbow and raking in the money. They are potters but they put on great airs about their glazes and kilns. To hear Lorenzo talk, della Robbia work is a child's mudpies in comparison." Basilio rubbed his head from crown to nape. "Lorenzo was the fair-haired hope of the family, but he had an inconvenient urge for the big city. Uncle and all tried to keep him in his place, but he wanted to paint, not pot, and there was no help for it. Off he went to seek his fame and fortune."

"And did he find it?" inquired Nicholas.

"Not at first. He took a job in a pottery workshop here to keep the wolf from the door. That was no difficulty since he had all his guild papers from Faenza in order, but it hurt his pride a bit. He turned out quite a lot of work, too, before his first fat patron dropped in his lap. Finally, his luck turned and a dried-up cardinal hired him to do a set of plates as a gift for a friend. Only, about the time the first plates were finished, so was the cardinal. The friend came to the workshop to see about her property, and presto! She decided to be Lorenzo's friend too."

"This lady," Nicholas inquired, "was la bella Giulietta?"

"Was she ever! Lorenzo thought he'd died and gone to heaven."

"I can well imagine."

"You know her?" Basilio asked with surprise. "You English aren't as quiet as you seem."

"It's about Giulietta that I'd like to speak to Lorenzo."

"He hasn't seen the woman in weeks, you know. They broke it off halfway through the portrait he was doing of her. Money, people said. Nearly always works out to have something to do with money. So, then she picked up with the baby Borgia and Lorenzo went back to seeking fame and fortune."

"Do you think he would want his old place back now the position is vacant?"

"Now, I hadn't thought of that," said Basilio. He paused a moment and stroked his head reflectively. "The lady may want her portrait finished after all. No, on the other hand, he wouldn't have time. He's got a big commission now, and no time for ladies. Giulietta requires a great deal of concentration from a man. Maybe after he gets paid, though. . . ." Basilio's voice trailed off in thought.

"Where can I find him?"

"At this hour?" Basilio rubbed his head. "In his workshop. It's halfway up the Street of the Five Moons. There's a sign of an angel over the door.

You won't be able to miss it."

"You're a treasure, Basilio," said Coffin.

Basilio took the silver the alchemist offered him and nodded placidly in agreement.

"Any other artists you'd ever like to know about," he said, "you know where to come to ask. That Buonarroti fellow, now, I know who broke his nose for him. Arguing about football, he was. These young ones are wild, that's all. I don't suppose any of them will amount to a handful of beans."

"You're probably right, Basilio," the Englishman replied, "but keep listening to them just the same."

The Street of Five Moons was across the river from Basilio's fragrant quarters, one of a network of streets climbing up the steep Capitoline hill. As the graverobber had told him, halfway up the street was a narrow housefront that sported a painted sign over the door. By the outline against the night sky, Coffin made out the silhouette of an angel, wings and trumpet included. Though it was nearly midnight, the front window still showed a light.

With caution born of habit, Coffin peered into the window before trying the door. Inside, an apprentice slumbered at the work table, head pillowed comfortably on his arms. Beyond him, an open door showed where work still went on in one of the inner chambers. Bright lamplight spilled out into the larger workroom and a shadow moved from time to time, telling of an occupant invisible from the angle of the window.

Methodically, Coffin tried the window and found it latched. He moved to the corner of the house and slid into the narrow passage that separated it from the next building to the left. No windows were wasted on the side wall, but the passage brought him out behind the building into a wide alley. He stepped around the heap of garbage in the gutter just behind the house and climbed the stone steps to the rear door. It, too, was latched, but the shuttered window beside it was not.

Carefully, Coffin opened one shutter a few inches and peered inside.

From this angle, he could see into the inner room more easily, but whoever worked there was only visible when a wrist and hand holding a brush came forward into the field of vision. All Coffin could clearly see from this vantage point was an easel with a mounted panel upon it. The lamplight fell squarely upon the panel painting, making it visible even from Coffin's position. From time to time, the artist's hand reached out and applied more color to the panel, but it was obvious the work was nearly finished.

Vivid in the lamplight, swan-throated and sloe-eyed, Giulietta looked out of the painting into the cluttered room. One perfectly plucked eyebrow raised, as if in surprise at her inappropriate garb, she stood in the blue robes of the Virgin Mary, holding a rigid but rosy-cheeked Christ child.

Coffin raised an eyebrow back at her, and went to knock at the front door like a gentleman.

His knocking roused the apprentice, who opened the door for him, knuckling his eyes. Coffin introduced himself and the boy disappeared into the inner chamber. The alchemist looked about for a brief moment while he waited for Lorenzo.

Before his nap, the boy had been grinding pigment, as the mortar and pestle on the table witnessed. From the size of the heap of powdered ocher he had prepared, Lorenzo's commission seemed large indeed. The corners of the room were stacked with paintings, framed and unframed, and the floor was littered with wood shavings left from their preparation.

The apprentice emerged from the inner chamber, followed by a slight young man in a smudged jerkin. The man gestured to a ladder connecting the work room with an upper chamber.

"Away with you," he said to the apprentice. "It's too late for you to be working. Go to bed."

The boy inclined his head respectfully and scrambled up the ladder with ill-concealed delight.

The slender man turned to face Coffin.

"Coffin is an English name, I believe. How may I help you, signore?"

For a moment, Coffin did not speak. The young man before him, he realized with a jolt, was the youth he had seen only that morning in Borgia's Trastevere palazzo.

He was wirier than Coffin would have guessed, seeing him only on the painter's scaffold. His wrists and hands were slender, and his mouse-brown, curly hair and deep-set eyes made it understandable that Giulietta had chosen him for pleasure.

Deduce, man, deduce, he told himself. Flamel said this would be child's play.

He realized the young man was waiting patiently for him to speak.

"Excuse me," he said. "I am sometimes subject to fits of abstraction. A terrible habit. Please accept my apologies. You are Lorenzo, are you not, the artist Cesare Borgia himself has chosen to ornament his personal apartments at his residence in Trastevere?"

"I am."

"If you would be so kind, I wonder if you could help me in a little matter I have been asked to look into. I would not for the world trouble you, not at this hour, but we do have an employer in common and I thought you would not mind helping one who also works for Cesare Borgia."

"Forgive me, signore, but I was not aware that his grace the duke had any Englishmen in his employ."

"His arm is long," Coffin replied.

"You won't find a man in Rome to argue that," Lorenzo said. He gestured Coffin to the apprentice's stool and drew up another for himself. Before he took the seat, he stood a moment longer and studied Coffin.

"Have we met before?" he asked.

"Possibly. I am a newcomer to Rome myself," Coffin replied indifferently.

"What may I do to serve you?" Lorenzo asked. "If it is another commission, I'm sorry, but as his grace knows, I am entirely too busy to oblige just now."

"No, not a commission," Coffin replied. "I merely have some questions to ask regarding a mutual acquaintance of ours."

"Not his grace?"

"Hardly. La Bella Giulietta."

Lorenzo stiffened.

"What sort of questions?" he demanded icily.

"Not personal ones," Coffin said in a soothing voice. "At least, not very. I was asked, you see, if there were certain things of which the lady was capable. It seemed to me you would be an excellent person to consult."

Lorenzo's eyes narrowed.

"I think you had better go. The hour is very late. Perhaps some other time—"

"No," Coffin said gently. "Now. Where his grace takes an interest, naturally the utmost urgency is required."

Lorenzo looked at Coffin, surprised by his tone. Their gazes locked. Coffin's eyes held his for a moment, then the Englishman raised an eyebrow.

"If my questions seem too personal, simply do not reply," he recommended. "I am no mind reader."

Lorenzo's face was set, but he replied evenly, "Go ahead."

Coffin realized he had seen that set expression before that morning. It had been when Lorenzo stared after Borgia for so long. Coffin paused meditatively, then asked, "Would you describe Giulietta as a jealous woman?"

"Jealous?" Lorenzo's expression relaxed into an unwilling smile. "Is an alley cat jealous?"

"I take it they're not. Did she have a temper?"

"Who doesn't?"

"She did?"

Lorenzo nodded.

"Did she ever lose her temper?"

"Oh, yes."

"With you?"

"Oh, yes."

"How?"

Coffin bent close to watch his face as Lorenzo considered his answer.

"Once," he reflected, "She threw my trunk hose out of her bedroom window. I had to bribe a servant to go out into the garden and search for them. But not until the next morning."

"Would you say she was vengeful?"

"I don't know. She doesn't hold grudges."

"In that case," Coffin went on gingerly, "do you think you might see her again, now that she's—available?"

Lorenzo did not answer, but the grim set returned to his lips.

Coffin nodded.

"I see. Just one more question, then," he said, as he rose from his seat. He stood over the painter and paused until the youth looked up at him inquiringly.

"Do you think she is capable of murder?" Coffin held Lorenzo's eyes with his own and saw the import of the question dawn. "Well?"

Lorenzo remained silent, but stared intently into Coffin's eyes. The Englishman lifted his eyebrows.

"I see."

He moved toward the door as Lorenzo rose to follow him.

"Thank you for your graciousness in receiving me at so late an hour," Coffin said. "I appreciate the value of your time. You will want to be at the scaffold ready to work as early as possible, I'm sure. It is an enormous task."

"It will be a masterpiece," Lorenzo said, eyes aglow. "It will be completed by midsummer without fail." He looked beyond Coffin into the future, all reserve melted. Almost without seeing the Englishman, he continued, "The entire hall and all the apartments off it are mine to decorate. The theme will be the classical heroes. There will be Alexander the Great, of course, with our Pope Alexander as model, and his son, our employer, will be Julius Caesar. The younger son, Ercole, will be his namesake, Hercules, and for the lovely Lucretia, it has not yet been decided—either the noble Lucrece or perhaps Judith with the head of Holofernes. By the time I am finished, all Rome will know my name."

"An impressive project," Coffin said. "I hope it will not be an inconvenience that Ercole Borgia died so unfortunately before you could do his likeness."

Lorenzo recovered himself and gazed sharply at Coffin. "Fortunately, I have done many studies of each of my subjects. And I paint very well from memory."

Coffin thought of the Madonna in the adjoining room and nodded, "I can well believe that."

"You will see when it is finished," Lorenzo said. His mouth was set once more. "Everyone will see."

* * *

In the street it was cold and misting. There was no way to tell in the darkness if anyone followed. Coffin paused once on his way home, certain he had heard a step behind him. There was nothing to be seen when he turned to look, and no other sound to be heard when he moved on. He squared his shoulders and clenched his icy fingers into fists to warm them. He contemplated detouring to the Sign of the Wolf to look for Angelo, but told himself that the little cutpurse had years of experience in looking after himself. In any event, if things had gotten out of hand since he was last seen, the crisis was well over by now. Besides, he reflected, if Angelo had gotten into something he couldn't handle, the chances were very slim that one lone and decidedly weary Englishman could do much to help.

Coffin shrugged, and took the short way home. Behind him in the shadows, footsteps followed.

CHAPTER FOURTEEN

The light in his room was still gray when he awoke. He had a vague notion that Costanza had come to him, some waft of scent that seemed to hint at her presence. He opened his eyes to the chill dawn light and blinked at the figure standing at the foot of his bed. There was a breath of scent, but not Costanza's clove and bay. This was a silken musk of ferns drowsing in warm woodlands. He rubbed his eyes, but the figure remained, a woman in a fur-lined cloak, hood pushed back to reveal hair as dark as the deeps of evening, silken ribbons binding it into a serpentine coil.

"Giulietta? he asked, unbelieving.

"You are slow to wake," she answered.

"I had not looked for such company," he apologized. "Did you come by night mare, moth, or dragonfly?"

"Ask your landlady," she replied. "Your little man Angelo told me where you lived. You are not the only one capable of bribing servants. I caught him out lurking last night."

"Nighttime is Angelo's natural setting, but Bianca must surely be harder to wake than I am at this hour," he said mournfully. "It must have been an inconvenience to rise so early."

"I never retired," she answered, pushing back her cloak so that the pale gauze of her evening gown gleamed in the pallid light. "I have questions to ask of you."

"Precedent is established for my undress, I hope?" Coffin asked, pushing back the sheets.

"As you wish."

He rose and pulled on a shirt. She eyed him coolly as he put on his hose and tied the points methodically.

"Are you more comfortable now? she asked.

"At this hour, the trick is to be less so," he assured her, and poured water from pitcher to basin, then splashed face and hands grimly and scrubbed himself red-faced. "Now, then. Questions?"

"You have been on Borgia business these last days, yes?"

"Yes."

"In the matter of Ercole's death, I have gathered."

"Again, yes."

"You undoubtedly realize he could have died at my hand."

"Yet again, yes."

"Englishman, let me be frank."

"My name is Nicholas, but by all means, be frank."

"Very well, then, Nicholas," she said, "though I had no reason under heaven to harm Ercole, you probably suspect me of wrongdoing."

"Go on."

"Last night I gave a dinner party for a number of fashionable guests, all of them gentlemen and scholars. Well, gentlemen or scholars," she amended. "One of the guests fell ill. He has recovered now, and seems quite himself, but at the time it was most unpleasant. Englishman, I cannot allow this to go on. It will not do. It simply will not do."

"Get a new cook," Coffin suggested.

"I have seen symptoms such as my guest displayed last night on one other occasion, signore." Giulietta's voice was cold.

"I thought you had," he retorted, the ice in his voice a fit match for hers. "I can tell you when."

She stared at him expressionlessly.

"I have been told how Ercole left you the morning after your, shall we say, last supper. Not very convincing. In fact, the last moderately plausible moment in the account I heard of that evening, was when your serving man sampled the meal for poison, found none, and was dismissed. After that, nothing is certain. I suspect, however, that you dined together and about an hour after you finished, possibly a little longer, but roughly an hour —Borgia died."

Giulietta regarded him as gravely as before.

"It was probably most unpleasant for you. As unpleasant, in fact, as it could possibly have been. But you are not a stupid woman, nor are you a naive one. On no account could his dead body be discovered in your house. You would die for it. So you hid the body until you could lay your plans. I don't know precisely what you did the next day— perhaps you procured the money to bribe your servants into silence. They are quite loyal on the whole. The man I questioned stuck firmly to your story. Borgia left in the morning, bright and early. But actually, you know, Borgia left that night. You had your men carry him to the river and drop him in. Common practice. Almost a family tradition, you might say."

"I wanted him to be found."

"But not in a shallow grave outside the city wall. Still, even there would be better than in your bed."

"I didn't kill him," she said, her voice soft and steady. "Nor did I poison that poor scholar last night. This must stop."

"Very true."

"Help me," she whispered.

"Tell me, then," he asked gently, "what that dinner was like with Ercole."

"We dined late, but the meal was not lengthy. The cook ruined what was to have been the last course. Ercole grew pale and said he had a headache. A little rest would help, I thought. We went up to bed. He unpinned my hair. He—"

"I know. Go on," Coffin said.

The woman gathered her composure and continued.

"He died in my arms. It was—" she broke off again but went on after a moment, voice nearly steady, "—unpleasant. Just as you said. Unpleasant. Everything else happened as you guessed."

"I see." Coffin sighed and covered his eyes with his hands. "Tell me about last night."

"What is there to tell? It was a dinner." Giulietta's voice rose slightly. "We dined early. We talked. The scholar began to rub his forehead and grow pale. I felt sure I was going to scream. It all began to happen again. It was like a dream—"

"Be calm," Coffin said curtly. "Start over and this time be objective. What exactly did you do last night that was the same as the night Ercole died?"

"Exactly the same?" Giulietta drew her perfect brows together until a single fine line appeared between them. "My cook, I suppose. The menu was different. I served my guests fish in a sharp wine sauce, chicken with almonds, and little meat tarts."

"Stuffed with what?"

"Currants and pork. Nothing out of the ordinary. You could speak to the cook, I suppose, but it was all quite routine."

"What else was the same?"

"Well," Giulietta pondered, "nothing. The wines were quite different."

"You did dine in the same room, I suppose?" Nicholas prompted. "Yes? Good. The same room, the same furniture, the same cook."

"I dismissed my old food-taster. Last night one of the other servants did the tasting."

"Out of the same porringer you customarily use?"

"Yes."

"You were there on both occasions, of course,"

Nicholas nodded. "What else? The cutlery?"

"Yes, I used the same silver. The wineglasses were the same, though I used more, naturally. And instead of just the two plates, I used the full set of six."

"Same plates and glassware. Have we left anything out? What about lighting?"

"Candles in the chandelier and sconces, all as usual."

"Good. Now, what did the man who fell ill do that Ercole did?"

"He ate dinner in my company," Giulietta said sharply.

"So did your other guests, and they suffered no ill effects."

"Oh, for heaven's sake! How should I know what he did or didn't do? I didn't stare at him like a serpent. He ate the food, he drank the wine—"

"Don't be impatient," Coffin scolded gently. "Something he did was the thing Ercole did—the fatal thing. We only need to work out what it was. Just be patient."

"I'm trying, but this is impossible," she snapped.

Coffin paced the length of the room and back.

"It's not impossible. It's inevitable. Sooner or later, we'll find the common factor. You don't believe me? Wait here."

Coffin strode to the door of his workroom and opened it, vanished inside and reappeared a moment later with a flask. He held it up to the window to allow Giulietta to see the contents.

"What in the name of the Virgin is that?"

"Ercole's dinner, or part of it," Coffin replied.

"If you look closely, you'll see a green pigment just perceptible at the edges. Actually, it was much clearer when I processed it. It's faded quite noticeably since then. In fact, the entire sample has deteriorated considerably. Are you all right?"

Coffin looked up in surprise to see Giulietta sit heavily on the edge of his unmade bed.

"You seem a little pale. Is there anything I can do?"

"I'm fine," Giulietta replied faintly, "only put that thing away."

"But this contains a substance, possibly barium salts, that may be the poison that killed Ercole. Do you see? If we can find what—or who—put that in the food, we'll know who the killer is. If your guest was given the same poison, the chances double that I can learn how it was done."

"I see."

"So it's very far from impossible. It's almost a matter of time alone."

She made a small gesture of desperation. "Put it away, *please*."

"Certainly," said Coffin with a perplexed shrug. He returned the flask to his work room and came back to sit beside Giulietta.

"Are you quite sure you're all right?"

"I'm fine. Obviously, what we must do is have you question my guest. He spent the night at my house and should still be abed. If anyone noticed anything about what sort of meal he made, he is the obvious candidate to ask."

"Or, more simply still, I could examine the dining room itself. Did you have the dishes cleared away, or did you leave things as they were?"

"Everything was cleared up as usual."

"Unfortunate. I'll also have to speak to your cook."

"Very well."

Coffin pulled on his doublet and quickly laced it, then put on his soft boots and took his cloak from its hook. Throwing it over one shoulder, he unlatched the door and threw it open to find himself face to face with Costanza, eyes wide and one hand raised to knock.

She blinked and parted her lips to speak, then looked past Nicholas to the slender woman behind him, seated on his bed. Nicholas saw the color rise into her face and then fade. She closed her lips and pressed them together firmly, but Coffin saw the tremor that brushed them. Without a word, she turned and vanished back down the stair.

Motionless, Nicholas watched her go, then heard the rustle of Giulietta's gown behind him and caught a breath of her musky scent.

"Since the worst seems to have befallen," she said, "perhaps we should take a moment to make the best of things. Little is worse, after all, than being punished for a crime of which one is innocent."

Nicholas turned to face her. "I can hardly believe it of myself," he answered ruefully, "but I feel I should speak to your houseguest first. Although your suggestion is tantalizing as well as reasonable."

Giulietta sighed gently and looked past Coffin down the stair.

"She is lovely," she admitted, "as well as touchingly young. When she has lost that bloom, perhaps."

"Lady—" Coffin began in English, then stopped himself and began again in Italian, "Signorina, you know your bloom has no date, nor will it fade. Shall a lily envy a gilly-flower?"

"You are gallant, Englishman, but your eyes speak more clearly than your words. We will go to my houseguest."

"So our actions speak more loudly than eyes or words," he concluded, and his face was touched with some regret.

CHAPTER FIFTEEN

Giulietta swept into her villa as briskly as the chill morning breeze. Her grief and uncertainty vanished, she came down upon her staff like a wolf on the fold, sending them to their appointed tasks like scattered lambs bleating after duty.

Coffin spent fifteen minutes with the cook and emerged from the kitchens convinced that she had neither the malice nor the acumen to introduce a poison undetectable to a taster into the meal. A similarly brief conversation with the servant who had acted as taster for the previous night's dinner elicited the same account Duccio had given. The food had been served forth, each course in its proper order, and duly sampled from the serving dish. On his dismissal, the taster had gone to the kitchen in search of his own dinner and had spent the time until he was summoned to clear up the dining room enjoying his meal and flirting with the cook. Coffin repaired to the dining room. Giulietta located him there after a routine inspection of her houseguest. The Englishman had surrounded himself with a litter of cutlery, wineglasses, and plates.

"I hope you approve," she said, as Coffin squinted at the window through one of her wineglasses.

"Yes, I do," he said, replacing the wineglass among its fellows on the table. "Wholeheartedly."

He selected a piece of silverware from the confusion and held it out to her. "What's this?"

Coffin pointed to the pronged tip of the implement. It was a palm's length, less than a finger's thickness. From the slender shaft, two tines sprang, evidently to be used at some point during a meal.

"That," Giulietta informed him, "is a fork."

"I never heard of it."

"You will. It's to eat with."

"I deduced that, but to eat what?"

"Almost anything. By spearing a morsel of food on the prongs, the food can be lifted to your mouth without dirtying your fingers."

"My fingers are usually clean enough to eat from," Coffin informed her. "Although I concede that such a device may be popular here in Rome, I doubt it will have any appeal in cleaner countries."

Giulietta frowned at him and he put the implement down on the table top, saying, "Novel, but hardly poisonous."

He lifted a plate and turned it over to inspect the back.

"This is the set of plates used on both evenings?" he asked.

"No," Giulietta gestured to the top shelves of the oaken china cupboard. "I used the set of six, there at the top."

Nicholas followed her gaze to the half dozen brilliantly glazed plates mounted as though they were objets d'art.

"You use those for meals?"

"Only very special ones. They were a gift from a friend. They are unique."

Coffin moved a chair next to the cupboard and prepared to mount it, then intercepted a look from Giulietta that prompted him to pause to remove his boots before ascending.

"You used all six last night?" Coffin asked. He peered closely at the shelf and reached out to take down the first plate.

"Yes," Giulietta replied. "Hand it down to me, carefully."

"There's a different picture on each one," Coffin observed with surprise.

"I told you they were special." Giulietta took the plate he offered from his hand and put it carefully on the table as he reached for the next.

Coffin paused and turned the second plate over. There was no guild mark on the back. He examined the front of the plate again. It bore a decorative border of stylized leaves, and in the center Venus and Mars were depicted in an intricate embrace. The first plate was adorned with a handsome young man embracing a tree. He now realized he had beheld Apollo and his true love, Daphne. The third plate showed Hercules in his lion-skin fondling a plump woman who wore nothing at all. Each plate he handed down to Giulietta portrayed a different legendary lover.

"My compliments on the invention these display," he said, handing down the last plate, that showed Neptune in an attitude of abandon with two mermaids. "Very educational."

"They were intended to be inspiring," Giulietta told him, setting the sixth plate in its place on the table.

"I daresay." Nicholas descended from the chair and put his boots back on. He surveyed the table carefully, hands on hips.

"So," he continued, "we have a poisoned man. I know he was poisoned, because I looked him over. I know he was poisoned at dinner, because that's where I found the poison. Don't look so pale, madonna. I won't go into unnecessary detail. So, somehow the poison found its way into his meal, though the same food was not only sampled by a taster, but enjoyed both by your fair self and your servants. It was not poisoned in the serving dish, yet it was when it was served."

"It's impossible."

"Obviously not." Coffin moved around the table as he spoke. "Last night, out of six people, only one fell ill. The connection should be clear. When we find it, we'll know how it was done, perhaps, even who is responsible."

"Now that you've intimidated my servants and ransacked my dining room, perhaps you would care to speak to my unfortunate guest," Giulietta suggested.

"Yes, I think that now I would."

"Only now?" Giulietta asked, brows lifted.

"Now that I know what questions I should ask."

Giulietta led Coffin up the wide staircase and into a bedchamber he had not seen on his previous visit. There, in the darkened room, she presented her houseguest to the Englishman. The houseguest, swathed in bed linen and blankets, with a brick to his feet and a look of peevish disfavor in his close-set eyes, surveyed Coffin wearily.

"Yes," he said, "we've met."

"Signore Ludovico Falchi and I attended classes together in Bologna," Coffin explained, recovering from his surprise somewhat. "His career since has been more successful than my own."

"In some areas," Ludovico remarked acidly, and closed his eyes.

Coffin looked down at Costanza's husband and tried to feel charitable.

"I have a few questions—" he began.

Falchi opened his eyes with an expression of utter boredom.

"I have been deathly ill. Must I be subjected to this?"

"You have been ill," Coffin agreed. "It is precisely what made you ill that I would like to question you about."

"You have no authority to question me about anything." Ludovico's voice was flat.

"But I will, just the same," Coffin said softly.

Ludovico shrank back against his pillows involuntarily.

"Would you use force against a sick man?" he

asked, then turned to appeal to Giulietta. "Madonna, I don't know what possessed you to admit this unscrupulous barbarian to your house, but I beg you to remove him before I suffer a relapse."

"Do that," Coffin smiled unpleasantly. "I don't mind asking questions of a corpse."

"Still at your filthy modern practices, eh, Englishman?" Ludovico sneered, his energy belying his plaintive words of a few moments before.

"Stop bickering," Giulietta ordered crisply. "No one enters my house without my express invitation. The Englishman is here, therefore I want him here. He will not leave until he has accomplished his purpose. Part of his purpose involves questioning you, Signore Falchi; therefore he will question you. He will question you. Do you understand?"

Both men regarded Giulietta in silence for a moment.

"*Quod erat demonstratum,*" she added, "as you scholars would say."

Coffin turned back to Ludovico.

"I think she made that quite clear," he said.

Ludovico curled his lip but said nothing.

"Last night you attended a gathering here, among a most distinguished company," Coffin began.

"It was a rather simple affair," Ludovico sniffed, "although compared to the social circles you are accustomed to, I'm sure it was amazingly distinguished. We dined and discussed the loves of the classical gods."

"Ah, yes," Coffin said, "inspired by the dinnerware."

"I don't expect you to comprehend me," Ludovico replied scathingly, "but try not to interrupt me."

"Then try to be more specific."

"Very well," the scholar said coldly. "The assembled company chatted about the classical gods, specifically as their qualities suggested the gifts and professions of each of the guests. Then, those of us who were able," he nodded graciously to Giulietta, "discoursed upon the gods and goddesses while the other guests stuffed themselves. You, my dear Giulietta, were absolutely charming in your discussion of the adventures of Venus. I, of course, was scintillating, although my topic, strictly speaking, was not that of a classical god, but rather a hero. Hercules, you know, was born a mortal."

"Wait," Coffin said, holding up a hand.

"The other guests, unfortunately, were fatuous in the extreme. Most of them had the good sense to keep silence and let their ignorance be guessed at, but the abominable Count Pitti persisted in parading his intellectual shortcomings."

"Ludo—"

"To be quite honest, when I experienced the initial pangs of my illness, I was not at all certain that I was not simply suffering from acute disgust inspired by Count Pitti's conversation," the scholar went on in a confiding tone.

"Shut up, Ludo." Coffin turned to Giulietta.

"My lady," he asked, his voice perfectly calm but his eyes ablaze, "Can you recall whether your guest of a few nights ago did or did not use the plate depicting his namesake?"

"Ercole?" whispered Giulietta. "Yes, I remember. When he saw the table with the new plates, he said it might have been made for him."

"Jesus, Mary, Joseph, and all the angels," Coffin said in English. Both Ludovico and Giulietta regarded him curiously. He shook his head and returned to Italian. "Then the next question is an easy one. Where, my beautiful Giulietta, did you get those plates?"

"They were a gift from Cardinal Buoninsegna, a well-wisher of mine."

"Where did he get them?"

"He had them designed by a young man from the north. He is quite talented, as you saw from the plates themselves."

"Rumor has it the Cardinal did not live to see his gift completed," Coffin observed.

"Despite his patron's death, the artist completed his commission." Giulietta lifted her chin as she spoke, her throat more than ever resembling a swan's. "The last plates were finished only a month or two ago."

"Before or after you rejected the artist and took another lover?"

Giulietta's lips tightened.

"After," she said.

Ludovico looked from her face to Coffin's, perplexed.

Coffin ignored him, taking Giulietta by the shoulders and turning her toward the door.

"Then, with your permission," he said, "I will take that plate and examine it."

"But how could a plate—" she broke off, puzzled.

"How else? How else could the poison have come to be there? We found it, madonna. The fatal thing Ercole had in common with Ludo here."

"It's true I only used it those two nights," she said. "Yet even if such a thing could be done, I simply can't believe Lorenzo would be capable of such a thing. We quarreled and parted. He's forgotten me long since."

"He has not."

"You know him?" Giulietta's brows shot up. "But—"

"I have spoken to him of you. Lorenzo has not forgotten you." Coffin thought of the painted Giulietta in her blue robes, looking out into the cluttered studio. "He hasn't forgotten anything."

"I don't know what you're talking about," Ludovico broke in, "but I think I deserve an explanation."

"But you've never gotten what you deserve, have you, Ludo?" Coffin reminded him sweetly, and left the room.

From Giulietta's house, Coffin took a route that tended homeward precisely as long as it took him to spot the men who were following. Once lulled into believing his destination to be one they knew, the pursuit grew careless and Coffin lost them with a minimum of effort. Doubling back, he made north toward Flamel's, cradling the Hercules plate tucked into his doublet.

To his surprise, although all the usual latches were unlocked, Flamel was nowhere to be found. Even his workroom overlooking the garden was deserted, the air untainted by even a stale wisp of smoke. Beside the window, the table was empty save for one book with a dagger between the pages to mark a place.

Warily, Coffin crossed the room and put the Hercules plate down next to the book so he could examine the volume more closely. No title was stamped on the spine, and the volume seemed to be composed of bound blank pages someone had written a sort of journal in, mixing French and Latin freely. Several shades of ink had been used, and the cramped, erratic writing looked as though the penman had seldom troubled to trim the nib of his pen. Several of the pages had roughly drawn maps and diagrams of buildings and machines. Coffin scanned the contents swiftly and concluded that he held one of the notebooks Flamel had kept on his travels. Cocking an eyebrow, he turned to the pages marked by the dagger.

Halfway down a page, the word barium caught his eye and he read on rapidly, translating as well as he could from the bilingual text and the irregular penmanship.

Barium, the crabbed calligraphy informed him, was found in the east in deposits of silver-colored metal. Compounds of the substance's salts were most useful, being employed in forging metal alloys, firing ceramics, and constructing fireworks. Several of the compounds had been found to be toxic, so great care was taken, the text went on, whenever the substance was employed. Also to be seen in this region of the Orient was a most remarkable variety of bear. One could come upon them in the mountains, eating not meat, but tender shoots of plants. The coats were unmistakable, half black and half white, with white heads marked with black eyes and ears.

Disgusted with that last bit of patent nonsense, Coffin shook his head and closed the book with a snap. It appeared Flamel had been quite certain all along that barium was the substance he was looking for, and had allowed him to conduct his search for the method of administering the poison to corroborate his theory. Even now, Nicholas told himself sourly, the old man was probably observing him from some secret vantage point, dark eyes narrowed into slits by his silent laughter at how his conjectures had been proven. Goaded by this thought, he spoke aloud.

"It was child's play, of course, to deduce the vehicle for the poison. If I find your precious barium is the culprit in the case, it will be an amusing sidelight, naturally. But the vital thing is to prove that the substance found in Borgia's stomach, be it barium or beeswax, is the same as whatever is in the glaze on this plate." He took up the plate and tucked it back into his doublet, cradling it carefully in the crook of his arm. As an afterthought, he picked up the discarded journal and slid that in too. It might prove amusing if he ever had time again to be amused. "Thank you for your trouble," he said, addressing the empty room and beginning to feel a trifle sheepish about it. "It has been entertaining."

From somewhere in the air around him he thought he detected a faint wheeze, almost of annoyance, then realized it was merely a draft soughing around the door he had left ajar. He took the hint, and departed.

CHAPTER SIXTEEN

Coffin unlocked his door and slipped inside only to pause in mid-stride and lean heavily against the wall.

"I didn't expect to see you here," he said.

Costanza rose from her seat on the edge of the rumpled bed, clasping her hands before her nervously. She glanced down at the large hamper resting at her feet.

"I only came to ask your advice," she said defensively. "Ludo never came home at all last night. I don't know what to do."

"Any other day I would advise you to have your locks changed. Today, I can assure you Ludo is fine. I've seen him."

"You?" Costanza's eyes widened. "Where is he?"

"At the house belonging to la bella Giulietta."

"That strumpet," Costanza interjected.

"He attended a dinner there last night where he

159

was inadvertently poisoned. Unfortunately, the dosage was not fatal, and his hostess sought me out on his behalf, which explains her early call on me this morning. Your husband is enjoying ill health at the moment, but he should be home soon, making you wait on him hand and foot."

"Oh," Costanza said flatly. She looked down at her hands again. "That's a great relief to me. I— thank you. I'll just be going, then."

"Did you bribe my landlady to let you in and force Tranio to carry that monstrous large basket of food all the way over here, just to ask me that?" Coffin asked. "Well, perhaps you needed the food to keep up your strength."

"My behavior is irrational, I know," Costanza snapped, tossing her head. "Such things are very contagious."

"A surprising word for Ludovico Falchi's wife to use," Coffin noted. "Perhaps you've been listening to me talk about Eristostratos."

"I've listened to you talk about a great many things," Costanza said. "But now, I think I shall leave."

Coffin moved to lean against the door.

"I think you shall not," he said gently. "Not until you have heard me a little longer. Costanza, I have had no time for seductions lately, but believe me, if I did, yours would be the first I would undertake."

"Don't be stupid!" Costanza flared. "I don't care what scandalous whores you sleep with! At least, not at the moment. Although it would be extremely upsetting to lose my husband and my lover to the same woman." She scowled fiercely up at him for a moment, then continued.

"What makes me angry is that string of lies you told me—how it was too dangerous to let me know what was troubling you! You just don't trust me. That painted little strumpet knows—if she was afraid for Ludo's sake, she would have gotten a doctor to see him. No, she knew. Oh, she knew just how to get it out of you—"

"My dear—"

"Oh, Niccolo! Why can't you trust me? I worry myself sick over you. You're coming and going all hours of the day and night, you wear a doublet twice as expensive as the rest of your clothes until it collapses into wrinkles, you don't eat, you don't sleep—you don't do anything you usually do—" Costanza gestured toward his workroom. "There is dust on your books, did you know that? Why? Niccolo, what's wrong!"

"My dear, I stumbled on to a most unfortunate situation. My studies, and my accursed curiosity, led me to examine a dead man. A murdered man. Now, I've been connected to the murder. Unless the real killer is discovered, I'll be blamed."

"How can they do that? If you—examined him," Costanza paused before the word, knowing only too well what it involved, "they could punish you for that, of course. It's a sin to—"

"Yes, yes. We've discussed all that many times." Nicholas nodded impatiently.

"Well, it is against the law to do what you do—but it isn't murder. They can't ignore one crime you committed in favor of one crime you didn't."

"They can do exactly as they please, I'm told. They cannot afford to let the murder go unavenged. Someone will have to pay the penalty. I would have paid by now, except that I managed to persuade them that my study of the body could lead me to the real assassin."

"Did it? Have you found the killer?"

"I have been spending all my time looking. Now, can you understand my behavior?"

"Yes, if all this is true, but I can't believe anyone could blame a murder on an innocent person. . .well, a nearly innocent person. Rome may be a city of little justice, but it does have order. No one can simply declare a man's guilt and kill him."

"I suspect their program will be the reverse."

"That's unthinkable."

"To Cesare Borgia?"

Costanza's eyes widened.

"I see you are thinking of it," he remarked.

"But—can't you find out who did it?"

"I was given until the funeral to do just that."

"Tonight! Ercole Borgia's funeral is tonight," Costanza protested. Her eyes widened further. "Niccolo! You cut up Ercole Borgia and studied him?"

"I couldn't resist."

"Oh! Oh, but my dear! They'll kill you!"

"Yes, I know," said Nicholas.

Costanza opened her mouth to speak again, but she was cut off by a stealthy scratching at the door. Coffin turned to open it.

"No, don't!" Costanza cried.

Coffin looked out the door and down into Angelo's face.

"What good instincts you have, my dear," he said over his shoulder.

"Maestro, I just came to warn you. Those four friends of ours are outside. They know where you live."

"Angelo," Coffin said wearily, "everyone knows where I live."

Angelo looked past him into the room and nodded to Costanza.

"How do you do, madonna? Is that a basket of food?"

"I should have thought you could buy your own food with the money La Bella Giulietta gave you to tell her where to find me."

"It wasn't worth that much to her," Angelo confessed. "Can I come in?"

"Yes, of course. Bianca's probably listening to every word. Get in here."

Coffin latched the door after Angelo entered, making straight for the hamper.

"Through no fault of your own," Coffin continued, "taking that bribe was the best night's work of your life."

"Are there figs in this little crock, madonna?" Angelo asked, oblivious to Coffin. "May I open it?"

"If it is of any interest to you," Coffin said dryly, "I am reasonably certain I have discovered how the crime was committed, and who arranged it."

"Would you like one?" Angelo asked Costanza, holding out the open crock of figs.

"Yes," said Coffin genially, "Amazing but true. I have saved both our skins through my deductive genius. It may surprise you to know, Angelo, that I was planning to tell Borgia that you were the killer if I failed to solve the crime."

"Oh, are these olives?" Angelo exclaimed. "I'm very fond of olives."

Coffin unlaced his doublet and withdrew the Hercules plate from its place of concealment under his arm. With a disgusted look at Angelo and Costanza, who were both bent intently over the basket of food, he raised the plate high and dashed it to the floor with all his strength.

Shards scattered everywhere.

Angelo and Costanza looked up from the hamper, stunned.

"Honest, Maestro," Angelo protested, "I only ate one."

"Please forgive me for distracting you," Coffin said, kneeling and starting to gather the splinters of earthenware, "but I am about to prove who killed Ercole Borgia and how. You may, if you wish, be of assistance."

"Of course, Niccolo," Costanza said, "just tell me how."

"Well, first I need to get all these bits of pottery together, and then I'm going to need roast mutton—"

"There's some here in the basket, Maestro," Angelo informed him brightly.

"—And some mussels in wine, and let's see—" he paused for a moment before he continued, "oh, yes, partridges in some kind of sticky sauce. One partridge will do I suppose."

"Niccolo?" Costanza asked dubiously, "Are you sure you wouldn't just like a little roast mutton?"

"And some olives?" offered Angelo.

"The roast mutton will do for a start," Coffin agreed, gathering up the last shard. "Bring it into my workroom. Angelo, you see Signora Falchi safely home and bring back the food as she prepares it. And don't sample any!"

"Whatever you say, Maestro."

Angelo led the way out the door, but Costanza turned back in the doorway.

"Darling?" she began anxiously, "are you quite sure—"

"Not yet," he replied absently, gazing at his handful of splinters, "but I soon will be."

CHAPTER SEVENTEEN

Well after sundown, Coffin emerged from his workroom. On the table in the outer room were the platters and serving pieces that had been used to serve forth mussels in wine and partridge in sweet sauce for the benefit of his flasks and vials. On the bed, Costanza drowsed. Angelo perused the remaining contents of the food hamper in one corner. Coffin rubbed the back of his neck wearily and seated himself on the bed beside Costanza. She stirred and opened her eyes to look at him questioningly.

He nodded and held out his hand to her. Across the palm lay a long shard of pottery. She took it from his hand and examined it cautiously.

"That's my proof," Nicholas told her. He sighed and rubbed his neck again. "Ercole Borgia was killed because he ate off a plate with poison in the glaze. To be precise, he ate mussels in wine sauce. There's something about the acidity of the wine that leaches out the poison more quickly. The splinters I tested with the mutton and the partridge showed much less of the substance. Every sample I took, in fact, showed less of the poison than I found in the contents of Borgia's stomach. I'll be willing to wager most of the glaze leached into the first food that was put on the plate, and there was less poison to seep into last night's dinner. Though now I think of it, perhaps the food served last night was less conducive to the leaching action. Still, it was only a matter of time before Ercole dined off the plate—the poison was there, waiting. One meal, or two, or three—sooner or later he would absorb enough of the poison for the purpose."

"Why only a matter of time before he used that plate?" Costanza asked.

"It was made for him," Coffin replied. "Your husband pointed out that by rights, Hercules doesn't fit into the set. All the rest of the plates showed gods. Hercules was a hero included in the group because he was Ercole's namesake. The plate itself wasn't completed until Ercole began his liaison with Giulietta."

"Maestro," Angelo said from his corner, "the man was blue. Eating from a poisoned plate made him blue? What kind of drug is that?"

Coffin's eyes gleamed and he sat up straighter.

"Now, there you have an interesting point, Angelo. I've been asking myself that most of the day."

"I thought you were trying to find proof to save yourself," Costanza protested.

"I had the proof early this afternoon," Nicholas

said, deprecatingly, "it was quite routine to confirm my guess. But the blue tint—you didn't see it, Costanza—"

"No, fortunately."

"—Fascinating. What I'd like to do is to test the remainder of the poisoned glaze and see if it has the same effect. I'll wager it doesn't in a smaller dose. Ludo, for example, showed no signs of blueness at all, so possibly the change in skin tone isn't a property of the poison itself, but of the action. Let me put it another way. Perhaps the blue coloring was not caused by the poison, but was part of the poison's effect."

"How's that again?" Angelo asked blankly.

"Angelo, take a deep breath and hold it," Coffin ordered. He rose and began to pace the length of the room, hands clasped behind his back.

Angelo obligingly held his breath until his face reddened, then expelled a deep sigh and began to breathe again.

"You see," Coffin exclaimed, "there's so much we just don't know. Why did your face get red?"

"Because you told me to hold my breath," Angelo answered.

"I mean, mechanically. Why should not breathing make your face red?"

"People need air, Maestro."

"What about eating—food goes into the stomach—but then what?"

"Well, Nicholas," Costanza said, "everyone knows what happens after that. It goes—"

"Yes, but the food—what happens in the stomach to break the food down into the mush I found in Ercole's stomach? How does the body use the food? Where does it go? Into the blood? And where does the blood go?"

"Nowhere, Maestro," Angelo replied. "Everyone knows that. You just keep it."

"Have you ever cut yourself deeply? Did the blood just seep out? No, it pumps out. Put your hand on your wrist. Can't you feel it pumping? Now where does the pumping go if you haven't been cut?"

Angelo scratched his head. "You mean it moves inside me?"

"Yes, I'm sure of it. And I think it takes food and air with it, all through the body. Unless something happens to interfere, I think that's what becomes of the air we breathe and the food we eat. But in Ercole's case something happened."

"He died," Angelo said, brightly.

"Hold your breath again," Coffin retorted. "He died, all right, and quickly, from Giulietta's account of the thing. Suppose, just suppose, he died so quickly, something happened to the blood as it was pumping. Suppose the food in the blood, poisoned by the glaze on the plate, did something to interfere with the air in the blood? Do you know what would happen if you went on holding your breath, Angelo?"

"Of course, Maestro. I'd die, too."

"You'd turn blue, Angelo. If you don't breathe, you turn blue. I've seen it myself. At Bologna, one of the students in my logic class choked on a piece of meat at dinner. We held him upside down and pounded him, but before we got it loose, he was gray-faced and toning nicely into blue. An unforgettable color, let me assure you."

"I'm sure this is perfectly revolutionary thinking," Costanza said, with a frown, "and my husband would happily argue about it all night. But now that you know the plate was poisoned, shouldn't you find out who poisoned it?"

"Excellent point, fair lady," Coffin conceded. "As it happens, I know who poisoned it. The pleasures of conjecture will have to take second place to matters of survival. Angelo, do you know the Street of Five Moons?"

"Sure, Maestro. It's on the Capitoline hill."

"Right you are. Halfway up the street there is a house with the sign of the angel out front. I want you to find our friends outside and lure them away with your elfin charm. Take them there, to the Sign of the Angel. Show them some more of the scenic places in the city, but don't lose them. Just take the long way there. I'll go directly to the place and meet you there. I want to have a little conversation before you arrive with reinforcements."

"Conversation with whom?" asked Costanza.

"With Ercole's killer, Lorenzo di Faenza. When I have asked my questions, we will turn him over to Borgia's minions and let them do the tiresome work of transporting him to the formidable Cesare. I will then proceed to make Lorenzo's guilt evident to his victim's brother, and let the Borgia family do what it will."

"And me?" Costanza asked.

"Tranio is at home, is he not?"

She nodded.

"Then there's no help for it; you'll have to stay here. Angelo and I will both be occupied, and you can't go about alone at this hour."

"What if Ludo comes home and I'm not there?"

"Ludo is living beyond his means at the moment. Unless I am mistaken in him, he won't be home until his hostess dismisses him once and for all."

"Don't take chances," Costanza said, her dark eyes warm.

Angelo rose from his corner, clearing his throat.

"I'll be on my way, Maestro. Give me a few minutes to get their attention before you start. I'll meet you in the Street of Five Moons."

"Certainly, Angelo," Coffin said, abstractedly. He did not take his eyes from Costanza's.

Angelo let himself out. Coffin latched the door absently. Costanza left the bed and came across the room to put her arms around him.

"Can't you just tell Borgia where to find the murderer?"

"I want to speak to him first," Coffin replied.

"To tell him you've guessed his trick? Or to try to get more of his poison for your everlasting analysis?"

"Both," he answered simply.

"English idiot! Once he knows you've discovered him, what's to prevent him from silencing you?"

"Just me," Coffin replied mildly. "That's why I

explained it all to you so carefully. If anything should happen, I would appreciate it if you would see Borgia gets my solution."

"If anything should happen to you," Costanza hissed, "I will inform on this Lorenzo and watch while they draw and quarter him."

"That's my gentle lover," Nicholas patted her shoulder reassuringly. "I will treasure your words tonight. At times, Costanza, you make me feel quite at home in this strange city."

"You may be a foreigner, Niccolo," Costanza assured him, eyes snapping, "but if anything happens to you and Lorenzo is to blame—*vendetta!*"

"It's nice to have friends," he said, and leaned down to kiss her.

Before she caught her breath, he had unlatched the door and gone.

Lorenzo di Faenza lit a lamp and leaned close over his painting of the Madonna, scrutinizing the line of her jaw carefully. Intent only on capturing a perfect likeness, he turned his attention to the adoring angel closest to her, and touched his own jaw reflectively. The angel's curly hair and adoration-filled eyes were his own. Without moving his eyes from the painting, he reached toward the table nearest him, groping for the palm-sized mirror he used to compare his jawline with the angel's. It came to his hand as if propelled there.

Surprise in his face, he looked up into the cold, dark eyes of Nicholas Coffin. Tall, relaxed as a cat, the Englishman leaned over Lorenzo for a moment, deliberately too close, then reached out a long arm for a stool, pulled it near and gestured for the artist to take it. Lorenzo straightened, letting the mirror drop from his fingers. With great care, he placed the lamp on the table, then reached to take the stool and moved it beside the table. Coffin held the stool with one hand and clamped Lorenzo's shoulder with the other. Startled, the slender young man looked up into Coffin's grim face. He kept looking as he seated himself, a trace of doubt suggested as he bit his lower lip.

Coffin smiled tightly, "Good evening, Lorenzo."

Lorenzo nodded, a nervous dip of the head.

Nicholas released his shoulder and began to rifle swiftly through the articles on the table.

"Forgive me for my presumption," he said as he worked. "Believe me, I'll be brief."

"You are a very courteous thief," Lorenzo said, his voice sharp.

"*Zut*! Worse names could be called in present company," retorted Coffin.

Coffin left the table, walked to a shelf and began to sort through the clay jars of pigments and colored earths.

"What are you looking for?" Lorenzo demanded.

"Why, the poison," Coffin replied. "Or didn't you keep it? Did you throw it in the Tevere? If you did, you're guilty of dropping toxic substances in the river. Oh, I know what your defense will be. Everyone does it, you say. Well, true. Or you could use the excuse that the Tevere itself is a toxic substance, which is also very true."

Coffin paused. Clamplike, his hand came down upon one of the jars, its lid neatly sealed in place with wax.

"How strange. All your other jars have a smear of paint on the lid to show what color the pigment inside is. But this jar—" He cleared a space on the table with a sweep of his forearm and placed the jar in the center of the empty space. "—This jar has nothing on the lid. See ? No mark."

Quickly, he peeled the wax away from the lid with his thumbnail, watching Lorenzo's expression closely as he worked. When more than half the wax was strewn across the table top, he grasped the jar and rapped the rim firmly once on the table's surface. The lid sprang off and a handful of metallic powder spilled out. Lorenzo stiffened and Coffin looked up from the powder to meet his gaze.

"Very pretty," he remarked.

"An artist has many tools you laymen know nothing about. That powder is to be ground for pigment."

"Really?" Coffin pushed a forefinger through the silvery substance, leaving a small furrow behind. "You fascinate me. What metal can be ground so fine it can be suspended in oil and applied to a painting? What color would this unlikely pigment be? And why does the pigment bear such a startling resemblance to barium salts?"

"I don't know what you're talking about."

With the back of his hand, Coffin swept some of the powder back into the jar and pressed the lid in place, then slid it into his pouch.

"How Flamel would enjoy making your acquaintance," reflected Coffin, rifling through the table top once again. "Ah, what have we here? A length of stout cord. Just the thing. Put your hands behind your back, please."

"I think you must be mad. Why do you keep talking about poison—and who's Flamel?"

"Just an old man who rather enjoys liars," Coffin replied. "Though I doubt he'd approve of a murderer."

With the speed of a viper, Lorenzo shot up from his seat, striking at Coffin. Flinching back instinctively, Coffin avoided most of the force of the blow but let Lorenzo beyond his reach. The painter pounced on an earthenware jar of oil among his supplies and dashed the contents at Coffin, then threw the jar. Coffin ducked and kicked the stool across the room to entangle Lorenzo's legs as he made for the door. The painter spun in his tracks and lunged for the window.

Coffin tried to stop in midstride toward the door, hit the table and overturned it. Lorenzo picked up the stool and opened the window in a shower of glass. Reckless with haste, he went out head first. Coffin reached the sill in time to miss a grab at the artist's vanishing ankles.

The racket brought Lorenzo's young apprentice to the door where he paused, flush-cheeked with sleep and mouth agape, staring at Coffin.

"Burglars," Coffin said tersely, then grasped the frame of the shattered window and swung himself feet first over the sill and out into the alley.

The square of lamplight from the window showed enough alley mud to give Coffin the direction of the tracks. He raced after, down the alley and out into the street. At the corner, beneath a red lantern burning in the doorway, a bare-shouldered woman hissed and beckoned him into the house.

As he neared, a shriek of laughter came from a window above, a woman's giggle.

"A man without a cloak, curly-haired, quick, which way did he go?" he demanded.

"That him, dearie?" the woman's painted face wrinkled with amusement as she pointed. "Heading downhill for the river? Hurry, before he throws himself in."

She stooped a little with her laughter as he set off, long strides gaining rapidly on the figure fleeing down the street, the pale blur of his shirt occasionally glimpsed in the glow from the windows he passed.

A sudden thought brought Coffin to a sliding halt on the uneven paving stones. Whirling, he looked back. Beneath a red lantern, the woman stretched out her bare arms to a slight figure, cloakless, but with a dark tunic over his white shirt. With a stifled curse, Coffin sprinted back the way he had come. By the time he reached the red-lit door, he was breathing unevenly, but she didn't wait for him to speak. Face mottled with rage under the paint, she waved her empty hands palm up under his nose.

"He promised me twenty carlini if he could hide inside while I misled you. I sent my nephew out to lead you astray and when I turned my back, he pushed past me and now he's gone and I don't have a thing for my trouble."

Coffin dug a twenty-carlini piece from his pouch and dropped it into her palm. She seized it greedily and waved him on.

"Same alley he came out of, the cheater—"

Breath nearly recovered, he set off uphill again, watchful. At the mouth of the alley, he paused, then went on to take the next alley, to come out a few doors down from the Sign of the Angel on the Street of Five Moons. Almost before he rounded the corner, he dropped back into the shadows, peering out at the activity on the doorstep of the artist's house.

The apprentice tumbled out of the door as he watched, and under Lorenzo's direction, took up position beside the passage's mouth with a poker held poised to strike. Lorenzo vanished back inside and reappeared a moment later wrapped in a cloak. With a last admonition to his apprentice, he struck off up the street, toward Coffin.

Angelo, closely followed by four men in Borgia livery, emerged from the mouth of the passage. The apprentice swung wildly at Angelo, missed by an arm's length, and went down, engulfed by Borgia's men.

"Not him!" Coffin bellowed, as he sprang from his shadow, "Him!"

Lorenzo started like a hare and whirled. Coffin threw himself toward the youth, caught a handful of cloak, and jerked backward with all his strength.

Lorenzo gave a strangled cry, but the clasp snapped and Coffin found himself with an armful of cloak. Lorenzo sprinted away down hill with the alchemist in hot pursuit.

"Angelo!" Coffin shouted, as he shot past the scrimmage on the doorstep, "Follow me!"

Angelo rose from the melee, brandishing the poker.

"That way," he shouted, elbowing an assailant. "Follow me!"

He waded clear of the battle and gave chase.

Lorenzo had a lead of several yards when they came down off the hill like a rockslide. Holding the momentum the slope had given him, he cut sharply north and then northwest, Coffin hard at his heels.

The streets were surprisingly full of people, considering the hour, and the chase threaded its way precariously through them. Their speed attracted some attention, and some bystanders gave chase themselves.

Lorenzo could only hear his own gasping breath as he ran, and the pound of his boots on paving stone, but Coffin heard a gathering growl of voices from the rear guard, an ominous counterpoint to the squeaks and cries of those he passed in Lorenzo's wake.

The street they followed turned hard west, and they raced on. Lorenzo tripped a wineseller in a crowd and Coffin had to hurdle the litter of winecups and tray, with the wineseller crouched in the midst of it all, cursing. He regained his stride and rushed on, but the wineseller left his wares and followed, shouting.

The street dipped sharply down to the Tevere, where a watchman held the bridge, his lantern high on its pole. He began to turn at the sound of the oncoming shouts, but Lorenzo caught him off balance and sent him sprawling. Coffin stumbled over the lantern's pole and scrambled to recover his balance. The watchman scrabbled at his shoulder. Coffin planted his heels and swung him off, then paused for a split second, transfixed.

Ahead, across the bridge, the sullen hulk of the Castel Sant'Angelo loomed, a gargantuan black chess rook set down by the Tevere. In every window niche, on every crenellation, every available inch of the fortress blazed with light. Ringed in fire to mourn the passing of one of their own, the Borgia stronghold stained the night sky red with the thousands of oil lamps set ablaze to mark the funeral.

To the left of the bridge, Coffin turned to gaze up at the silhouette of old St. Peter's, high on the Vatican hill, its crumbling hulk a jumble of bell towers and courtyards.

And across the bridge, marshaled with all pomp and panoply to bear Ercole Borgia to his last rest, the funeral procession was assembled, ready to proceed.

The watchman grabbed at Coffin's arm again and the alchemist sent him sprawling. The rabble pursuing him had gained while he stood staring, and Lorenzo was now yards ahead and racing straight for the first rank of the procession.

He sprinted forward in a last burst of effort, straining to catch Lorenzo before he reached the cover of the funeral. He was still on the bridge when the deep bells of the city began, like ponderous stars coming out at twilight, to join the slow, deliberate tolling of the midnight hour.

Mournfully, the bells rang out, and the funeral procession began to move.

The rabble of pursuing Romans was almost on him now, but Coffin found one last surge of strength that brought him to Lorenzo's elbow. The artist was hampered by the press of onlookers across the bridge. He could not squeeze out of the path of the oncoming procession, so he turned forward again to merge with it.

The leading rank was composed of a troop of Indian Musselmen and an elephant. Lorenzo squeezed past one keeper, but a second felled him with a blow of the heavy elephant goad he carried. The elephant halted, unnerved by the disturbance, lifted its trunk and trumpeted.

Coffin careened into a keeper and tried to fight past, intent on reaching Lorenzo. The keeper swung his goad, but Coffin sprang aside and lunged inside the keeper's guard, pinned his arm, and took the prod away.

The elephant trumpeted again and began to pull back, dragging straining keepers in its wake. The shouting mass of Borgia's men, Angelo, and interested bystanders met the fringe of the keepers. Violence ensued.

Coffin took a stance over Lorenzo's inert form and laid about him mightily with the elephant goad, roaring, "Saint George and Merry England!" at the top of his lungs. A skinny Musselman shouted, "Scotland and Saint Andrew!" in reply, and sprang to cover the Englishman's back. Chaos spread outward from the knot of brawlers, until the onlookers ranked along the way shoved and jostled their way into the melee.

To the rear, order reigned. From the assembled ranks of the procession, men in the Borgia livery pushed forward, surrounding the brawl and pressing inward. For a moment, the surging fighters threatened to encompass the newcomers and expand the battle, but the Borgia line held. As the fighting calmed, the liveried guards drew apart to form a corridor through their midst.

Coffin, halted in mid-swing, lowered the elephant goad slowly as he watched the passage form. As though enchanted, the fighters froze where they were, all eyes on the corridor.

The tolling of the bells ceased.

Through the corridor in the throng, a single horseman came slowly forward. The horse was black, as were its jeweled caparisons. The rider was clothed all in black, with a sable cloak flung back from his shoulders. He was tall, broad-shouldered, and russet-haired. Beneath his heavy brows, his eyes glowed golden. As he drew forward, the crowd pressed back, straining away from the horse and rider. The rider guided his mount on, into the center of the frozen brawl.

He drew rein immediately in front of the tall Englishman, and rested his clenched fist in its jeweled gauntlet on his hip.

"Well, gadfly?" he asked, his voice rich as velvet.

Coffin stood, hands clasped over the butt of the elephant goad, and regarded Cesare Borgia, the most dangerous man in Rome. He shifted his gaze downward to where Lorenzo was beginning to stir at his feet, then looked up again to meet Borgia's gaze.

"I've brought you your brother's killer," he said simply.

Borgia held him with his heavy gaze for a moment, then flicked a glance toward Lorenzo.

"So," he said, his face expressionless, "the hunt is over." He turned to one of his men. "Take them to a chamber and guard them well." His head lifted, tossing his mane of dark red hair as he pitched his voice to address the crowd.

"The rest, disperse. My brother goes on to his rest."

Liveried men hoisted Lorenzo to his feet and pinned his arms behind him. Coffin was relieved of his goad and led away after the artist. The rest of the throng moved back to their places, and the elephant was led forward once more by its battered keepers.

Borgia turned his black horse back to make his way to his rightful place in the procession. A sudden movement made the stallion throw his head up in fright. Borgia's hands on the reins steadied the horse as he glared down at the culprit.

Almost beneath the great horse's hooves, a small man sprang up before Borgia, a smile on his pointed face.

"Your pardon, your grace," he said, impudent despite his bruises. "An accident. I won't do it again."

For a moment, the little man's hand rested on

the jeweled trappings of the horse's harness as though to soothe the beast. When he took his hand away, one of the gleaming gem rosettes came with it. Inclining his head obsequiously, the small man backed carefully away from the horse into the press of the crowd and vanished.

CHAPTER EIGHTEEN

In his anxiety to oversee Lorenzo's capture, Coffin ignored his own rough treatment. The pair were hustled into a bare-walled tower room with barred windows and a single door. There was a heavily carved oaken chair in the center of the room, two torches mounted on the wall for light, and a guard on the other side of the door.

With a defiant glare at Coffin, Lorenzo seated himself in the chair.

"Go ahead," Coffin said amiably. "Enjoy it while you can. One look down his nose will have you up and offering him the place with your tail wagging like a puppy."

Lorenzo rose.

"Then you take it," he said. "We'll see how long you keep him standing."

"Don't be an idiot. It's bad tactics to plead a case seated. I'll need to be on my feet when I explain what you've done. It will require all my concentration to remember the details."

"I don't know what you're talking about."

"I'll bet you don't. Better practice that voice of injured innocence if you expect to be convincing. Put more stress on 'talking' for a start. Try for a plaintive tone," Coffin recommended.

"First you break into my studio, making wild accusations. Then you drive me through the streets like some kind of criminal—"

"Don't be so vague. I know exactly what kind of criminal you are. And wasn't it odd for an injured innocent like you to run straight here? Odd place for someone to visit—unless you wanted to tell your patron about me before I told him about you." Coffin's voice was even.

"You're laughable," Lorenzo snapped. "Do you know whom you accuse? I am the artist singled out by Cesare Borgia to execute the most important commission in Rome. One day St. Peter's itself will be ornamented by my hand. Even if there were truth to your charges, do you think he would listen to you? Even if you had some proof, how could he believe you?"

"You have a high estimation of your own importance in the Borgia scheme of things," Coffin observed. "Did Giulietta agree when you told her of your potential?"

"Don't talk about Giulietta." Lorenzo glared at Coffin. "Don't even say her name."

"She quarreled with you—"

"Did she tell you that?" Lorenzo demanded.

"It's common knowledge."

"You're lying." Lorenzo took a deep breath and steadied his voice. "We argued sometimes. I wanted her to stop what she did, or at least stop treating it as if it were a profession. She never took money from me. Everything I gave her, those were gifts. She never asked me for jewelry. I don't know why she kept wanting more things; she had lots of beautiful things. But she wouldn't believe I could find patrons and keep her. I told her and told her. I could have given her things. I could have. I can now. We could be happy now."

"She wouldn't take money?" Coffin raised an eyebrow.

"She asked me to paint her portrait," Lorenzo said. He looked at his hands. "It was less than half completed when she told me she had found someone else."

"You finished it from memory?"

He nodded. "I haven't seen her since that day. I took the plates to her villa, but they told me she was out."

"Ah, yes. The plates," Coffin said.

"What about them?" Lorenzo looked up in challenge.

"Most ingenious." Coffin inclined his head. "I should think the temptation to take credit for the idea would be overwhelming. Especially since you'll be killed whether you confess or not. It was very clever of you."

"I don't know what you're talking about." Lorenzo looked down at his hands again and refused to say more. Coffin prodded him industriously for several minutes, then gave up and went to gaze out the window.

The silence held until the door latch clicked. A pair of uniformed guards entered, flanked the doorway and stood at attention. Over the threshold stepped Cesare Borgia. He paused, turned his heavy head to gaze at each of them in turn and moved toward the oaken chair.

Lorenzo got to his feet and stepped back from the chair, gesturing Borgia to seat himself. Borgia did so, then peeled off his elaborately jeweled gauntlets in silence. The guards stared fixedly at nothing. Only the shadows moved, thrown by the wall-mounted torches.

Lorenzo broke the silence first, throwing open his arms and kneeling at Cesare's feet.

"I desire only to serve you, your Grace," he began plaintively. "Tell me what I have done to be brought here a prisoner? What have I done to so displease you?"

"Much better," Coffin observed. "With a little practice you have made great strides."

Cesare turned his amber gaze to Coffin and curled his upper lip.

"Do not bray unbidden, Englishman. I will hear you when I wish. And you," he put his boot to Lorenzo's shoulder and pushed him away. "I do not care for dogs that fawn."

"All dogs fawn," Coffin reminded him. "It is their nature."

"Hold your tongue, gadfly," Cesare ordered with ominous evenness.

"Why did you come here, if not to listen to me?"

Coffin asked. "You asked for your brother's killer. Here he is."

Borgia looked at Lorenzo. The youth met his gaze squarely, head high despite his kneeling stance.

"Get up," he ordered. "Talk."

"Your grace, you know me. I have received your commission to decorate your own apartments in your palazzo. This foreigner has made wild threats and accusations against me, followed me, broken into my studio and rifled it, harassed me—"

"Harassed you?" Coffin cried, incredulously.

"Be quiet," Cesare said. "I selected you as a painter, Lorenzo, because of your skill. Your character is unknown to me. This man, whom I have asked to employ his learning on behalf of my family, tells me you killed my brother."

"Let him prove it!" Lorenzo challenged.

Cesare turned to Coffin.

The alchemist calmly produced his pouch and loosened the strings. He spilled its contents out and from among the silver pieces and the slender lock-picks selected a single splinter of earthenware, and the wax-rimmed jar he had taken from Lorenzo's studio. He handed both to Borgia.

"The jar," he informed him, "contains barium salts—I believe. I have not had an opportunity to analyze it. A compound of barium salts was used to poison your brother. The powder comes from your protége's workroom. The shard is part of a plate commissioned for your brother's mistress, the courtesan Giulietta. It was made for her by Lorenzo along with several matching plates. The others are perfectly innocuous. The plate this shard comes from portrayed your brother's namesake, Hercules. Lorenzo made and delivered the plate after he had been told by Giulietta that because of her liaison with your brother, she would no longer admit him to her house or her bed. Scorned by his mistress, Lorenzo devised a way to eliminate his successor. He designed a plate that would appeal to your brother's somewhat undeveloped artistic tastes and introduced into the glazing of the plate a toxic substance that leached into the food served to your brother when he dined with his mistress. Lorenzo comes from an accomplished family of potters in Faenza, as I'm sure you know. He is an expert on glazes. The same barium compound I found in your brother's stomach after his death appears whenever the glaze on this shard comes into contact with food, especially acidic foods, such as mussels in wine."

Cesare set the jar aside but turned the shard over and over in his hand, then raised his massive head to look at Lorenzo.

"Is this true?"

"That's not proof," Lorenzo cried. "That shard could be from any plate. The jar holds one of my pigments."

"You forget," said Borgia coldly, "I have no need of proof. My brother was killed. His killer will die, in his turn. The question of proof does not concern me."

"But, in the name of justice—" Lorenzo protested.

"It is justice that my brother's death be avenged."

"Listen to him!" Lorenzo snatched at Coffin's sleeve. "In a question of criminals, he's worse than I! He breaks the law as he pleases, just to suit his own ends."

"I am the law," Cesare reminded him. "All the law you will ever know."

"It isn't my concern which of you is worse," Coffin replied. "I only want to live through this. To do that, I had to find Ercole Borgia's killer. I have."

"But you haven't proved it," Lorenzo said frantically, "not really—"

"Perhaps," Cesare interjected, "he doesn't need to. You will confess, of course."

Lorenzo threw back his head in startlement.

"Oh, yes," Cesare replied to his surprise. "You will. It might take an hour or two, but certainly no more. Less if we use the rack, more if we use the thumbscrews. It would be a waste to ruin your hands with thumbscrews, but still, you'll have very little use for them after tonight, won't you?"

Lorenzo's eyes grew wild, his head strained back until the cords in his throat stood out. He tossed his head from side to side desperately, searching for some escape.

With a lunge, he moved to the wall and pulled a smoking torch from its socket and threw himself toward Borgia, striving to reach the door beyond.

The guards pulled him down as hounds attack a stag. For raising his hand against their master, they

let his life out on the stone-flagged floor. Cesare
stepped backward to avoid staining his boots with
the blood.

Coffin looked down at the ruined body and felt
a great coldness fill him. He walked with dream-
like slowness to the door of the chamber and
paused to look back.

Black-clad, impassive, Cesare Borgia stood over
the youth, one fist clenched over the pottery shard,
the other on his dagger. As Coffin watched, he released his grip on the knife hilt and lifted his eyes to
Coffin's.

"Englishman," he said, "I am grateful to have
my brother's death avenged. What payment will
you take?"

"My life," Coffin replied, "as we agreed."

"What more?"

"I am no creature of yours, your grace."

"Yet you were hand in glove with me in this,"
Borgia said, then added suddenly, "so take this
payment." With quick fingers, he pulled his
gauntlets from his belt. They were heavy with embroidery and glinting with gems. Stepping across
the body, he put them into Coffin's hand. For a
moment they lay there in his slack fingers, then he
took them.

"Many thanks," he said quietly. "My hands are
cold. These will be welcome."

Borgia took up the jar and examined it.

"So this is the poison that killed my brother."

"I believe so," Coffin nodded. He stretched out
a hand for the jar. "Still, it is necessary that I
analyze the powder."

Borgia gazed at him limpidly.

"Do not trouble yourself," he said. "The situation has been resolved to my satisfaction."

Coffin still held out his hand.

Borgia put down the jar and turned nonchalantly away. Coffin promptly placed the jar in his pouch and pulled the lacings tight.

"Should you have some interest in the matter, of course, you may pursue your studies," Borgia went on, disinterested.

"You are generous," Coffin responded coldly as he moved to the door.

"Stay a moment, Englishman."

Coffin paused and glanced back over his shoulder. With a small feline smile, Borgia flicked one hand in a gesture of dismissal.

"You may go."

Borgia watched him leave the tower, but no one followed him from there. Alone in the empty streets, he walked slowly, tugging on the gloves against the predawn chill.

Across the bridge, a small shadow detached itself from the gloom and came to walk beside him.

"Pretty nice gloves," Angelo remarked after a companionable silence.

"Wages of sin," Coffin told him.

"But it wasn't you that sinned, Maestro," Angelo reminded him. "Not in this case."

Coffin stretched his arms over his head and yawned hugely.

"You're perfectly right, Angelo," he said, when he recovered. "But I intend to go home and take Costanza to bed and sin repeatedly until Sunday mass. I will then confess, be shriven, and go home to bed and begin again. If Ludo doesn't like it, he can stay with Giulietta."

"Giulietta has higher standards, Maestro," Angelo pointed out.

"Then he can stay on as her taster. Good night, Angelo. I'm only sorry I can't give you what your help in this was worth to me."

"Oh, never mind that, Maestro," Angelo grinned. "Borgia paid me, too."

On his outstretched palm, the jeweled rosette from Borgia's stallion winked and glittered in the gathering dawn.

A Scene from *The Duke and the Veil,* The
Second Adventure of Nicholas Coffin,
THE ALCHEMIST.

For nearly a league they continued thus, Fenelon
in the lead, evidently following directions from a
scrap of paper he consulted from time to time, and
Coffin trailing lackadaisically behind with Angelo,
the pair staying just close enough to keep the
Frenchman in view. The sun beat down on their
shoulders, its heat intensified by the absence of any
breeze.

"Maybe he is going to Naples," said Angelo as
they trudged along. "He's headed in the right direction."

"He's been checking that paper he's got more
frequently this last quarter mile," Coffin replied.
"My guess is he's either lost or he's close to his
destination."

As if his words were a signal, Fenelon produced
the piece of paper once again, scanned it, and cut
sharply off the road, plunging into an overgrown
foundation of tumbled stones. Warily, Coffin and
Angelo followed.

Fenelon's path was clear enough through the
weeds and undergrowth, but when they entered the
heart of the ruin, there was no trace of their quarry.
Wordlessly, the pair split up and began to search
the sprawling mass.

"Here," exclaimed Coffin, after several minutes of silent scrutiny in one corner of the ruin. Angelo crossed the foundation and leaned over the Englishman's shoulder, while Coffin knelt at the top of what appeared to be a steep flight of steps extending below the foundation.

"A wine cellar?" Angelo asked.

Coffin pointed down to a weed straggling from a crack between the steps. A stone lay across the weed's stem, but all the leaves were still green and unwilted.

"Not long," Angelo nodded. "Not long ago at all."

"Clumsy of him," Coffin agreed. He undid his pouch and produced his flint and the packet of fine wood shavings he used to strike a light, then brought out the parcel of candles from his doublet.

"Now we know why he stopped for these," he said, dividing the candles with Angelo. "You watch this stair, and stop him if you see him come out and don't like the expression on his face. I don't know where these steps lead or whether there are more entrances, but do the best you can. If anyone other than Fenelon comes out, or me, of course, hold him until I join you. Got it?"

"Got it," Angelo replied. "What do you think is going on down there?"

"A meeting, arranged despite a great deal of trouble," Coffin answered, striking his spark and blowing it into a flame healthy enough to light his first candle. "I do hope I won't be late."

Shielding his candle flame with one cupped hand, Coffin padded down the treacherous steps and vanished into the darkness. His first steps into the gloom were quick, almost a spring. Noise would not betray him any more swiftly than his candle would if he were observed. His best hope was Fenelon's eagerness to keep the appointment he had made.

Well within the mouth of the passage, Coffin backed into a niche in the wall and looked about him, every sense attuned. No desolated wine cellar this, the passage seemed to go on without widening for some distance. At intervals, shallow niches were set into walls of porous stone, marked everywhere by the stone worker's chisels. It was as though the tunnel had been scraped out of stone, a burrow winding away into the darkness and silence of the earth. Holding his candle high, Coffin scanned the niche he stood in, noting the whitewashed walls were painted with pale figures of shepherds and lambs, all flaking away with age. At shoulder level, the whitewashed stone had been gouged away and in the dark recess beyond something gleamed palely in the candlelight. Coffin looked more closely, into the hollow sockets of a skull, grinning to itself in the darkness. He started and hot wax dripped across his knuckles as he realized where he must be.

The good shepherd, painted on the wall above his head, smiled calmly at his flock while Nicholas picked up a bit of the stone torn away by the vandal who had exposed the skeleton behind the wall. Holding it close to his candle, he saw he held a fragment of plaster. Not all the walls were stone, then. The rear wall of each niche was likely to be

plaster, and behind each wall lay a sleeper, concealed here down the centuries, for he stood in one
of the legendary lost catacombs of the first Christians of Rome, who had hidden their dead from the
wrath of the emperors who persecuted them. Each
niche had been sealed with plaster and mortar to
conceal the body within, and the wall painted with
the symbols of their faith. As more Christians died,
more passages were carved, until the burial place
formed a maze, a city of the dead. Lost down the
drift of years, the dead had slept undisturbed, while
Rome burned and was rebuilt. In time, a Christian
emperor was crowned, and the empire built
basilicas and churches, and enshrined their martyred dead. But the catacombs slept on, through
the waning of the Empire and the slow dwindling
of the city through plague and warfare. The city
faded and forgot the martyrs, save only for legends
of Rome's hidden past.

Now, someone had found a door to the maze,
and had entered the city of the dead beneath the
city of the living. Someone had opened one of the
burial niches, and perhaps more, looking for riches
in the tombs of the forgotten Christians of Rome.

Coffin drew in a breath of the thin, stale air.
Fenelon was somewhere inside this maze. The
scuffed footprints in the dust at his feet told him
that, and his reason told him that the Frenchman's
scrap of paper had held directions, sent by someone who wished to rendezvous with Fenelon here
in the catacombs. Moving with a cat's deliberate
tread, Coffin left his niche and followed the footprints into the silent passage, pausing when he

reached a branching. To right and left, tunnels extended on the same level, but ahead the passage fell away into space. He knelt at the edge and held his candle down into the dark. There were handholds cut into the stone wall, but no need to use them, as the drop was bridged efficiently by a modern wooden ladder. Coffin eyed it warily but no rungs appeared to have been tampered with, and traces of dust and mud on the wood suggested it had been used recently. The looters must have made regular trips into the maze, Coffin reflected, to make such improvements worth their while. Holding his candle high and managing the rungs with his free hand, he clambered down, and picked up the trail again at the foot of the ladder. Here the air was noticeably poorer than on the upper level where the draft from the stair had provided some fresh air. As he moved along the passage, Coffin noted that as the air grew worse, the paintings on the wall grew better. The colors were unfaded in the paintings of doves and shepherds and parties of solemn feasters clustered around their tables laid with wine and spherical loaves of bread. How long had it been since the painters laid down their brushes, Nicholas wondered. A thousand years? Time hung about him like a mist here. How many slept here? How far into the darkness did the passages extend?

He walked on marveling, past crossing and branching, always following the fresh footprints in the dust, into new turnings that led down into more levels and more passages, web-like in the porous stone. Names and words were scratched into the walls among the bright paintings, and here and there gouges in the walls marked where tomb robbers had been, rifling the past. As he made his silent way past a painting of three youths in a fiery furnace, their hands held up in tranquil prayer within their flaking ring of fire, his eyes fell upon the path he followed and he saw another set of fresh footprints had joined those of Fenelon's.

Every sense straining, he stalked noiselessly on. The passage bent and broadened into a low little room, with a shelf set into one wall to serve as an altar, and passages opening into each of the other walls. On the wall above the altar was a painting of Christ driving a chariot, his head encircled in flame. Sprawled on the dusty floor before the altar was Fenelon, a dagger planted neatly between his shoulder blades.

Coffin stood in the passage and stared at the sprawling corpse, quick dark eyes taking in the candle with its blackened wick nestled in the dust beside Fenelon's left hand. In the candlelight, the blood stain around the dagger looked black against the fabric of the doublet. Coffin drew closer, free hand outstretched to touch Fenelon's slack fingers. How long ago had he died? Could the creeping chill of the catacomb have spread through the flesh already? As he bent, Coffin heard a swift intake of breath from the darkness at his back.

Cursing his carelessness, he spun, trying to regain his balance, but he was too late. Something struck him on the head and pain flashed white hot across his eyes and slid him down into darkness, unconscious in the dust.